TROUBLED WATERS

Jean Davidson

CHIVERS

British Library Cataloguing in Publication Data available

This Large Print edition published by AudioGO Ltd, Bath, 2013.
Published by arrangement with the Author
U.K. Hardcover   ISBN   978 1 4713 1937 2
U.K. Softcover   ISBN   978 1 4713 1938 9

Printed and bound in Great Britain by
TJ International Limited

CHAPTER ONE

Sally climbed over the last rocky outcrop and surveyed the white sand of what she now called 'her' beach. She had discovered it a few days ago when, eager to explore, she had walked round the headland that bounded the wide bay at Xora Village, found another headland further on, then another.

She had wandered on, sometimes knee-deep in the sea, for half-an-hour until she came to this stretch of fine sand almost unmarked by footprints. Bounded at the back by a low cliff of yellow sandstone, crumbling at the far end into a pile of boulders and rocks, it was quite private. Each day she had returned and had it to herself.

She took her towel out of her bag and tossed it on to the sand, wriggling out of her shorts and T-shirt and kicking off her sandals. The sea-breeze which had tangled her fine ash-blonde hair felt good against her skin which was sticky from the heat. She was looking forward to her swim.

Just here the sand shelved gently into the sea and the direction of the wind brought cream-topped waves curling on to the beach like mini-breakers. As Sally dived into them, the coldness of the water made her gasp.

She got used to it and swam steadily out

1

to sea before rolling over on to her back. A piercingly blue sky arched overhead, the sun was sparkling on the water, and for the first time in nearly a year she felt free and truly glad to be alive.

Reluctantly, she began to swim back to shore with her neat, effective crawl—the others would be expecting her—then, as the waves began to break over her, she wallowed in them, laughing out loud. Touching sand, she lay still for a moment to recover her breath, then stood up and slicked back her hair, wiping the stinging salt from her eyes.

'And just who the hell gave you permission to trespass on this private beach?'

Sally started and blinked in surprise. The voice was unmistakably American, the man young, lean and tanned. His thick brown hair glinted gold in the sun. He stood with arms folded, frowning at her.

'Private beach?' she repeated bemusedly. 'No one said—'

'Ignorance does not count in a court of law. And can't you see that sign up there?' He jerked a thumb over his shoulder. Sally lifted her gaze and saw a weathered, rusted signpost.

'It doesn't say "private beach",' she replied coolly. 'It says "No nude bathing". They're posted all over the place.'

The American permitted himself a tight smile. 'So you read Greek, huh?'

'Excuse me.' Sally tried to brush past

him. The sea water, drying on her skin, was beginning to chill her. 'I need my towel.'

He refused to give ground. 'Not until I have a few answers first. Who *are* you, for a start?'

*　　*　　*

Sally eyed his powerful build, the long legs in faded jeans. They were a long way from anyone else, and she was beginning to feel distinctly uneasy. 'I might ask you the same question. Jumping out and frightening me like that! Telling lies about private beaches.' She stepped around him as she spoke, determined to make a wide detour round him and regain her clothes, but he caught her arm.

'This *is* my beach, though I don't happen to carry the papers on me. I thought you'd fall for the signpost trick. Now, tell me, who *are* you?'

Anger triumphed over fear. Sally shrugged his fingers from her arm, picked up her towel and began to dry herself. 'My name is Sally Johnson—I'm a travel courier with SunSea. You can check in Xora, if you like. How about you?'

She was aware of his careful scrutiny as she pulled her clothes back on over her damp bikini—she would not be so foolish as to attempt to change in front of him. When he didn't reply, she went on, 'And if this is your beach, why haven't I seen you here before? Where's your house?'

3

He stepped menacingly close. 'That was a careless slip, Miss Johnson. So this isn't your first visit? Well, I'm warning you, it had better be your last. Do you understand me?'

It took every ounce of Sally's self-possession not to give way before his anger. His threatening stance intimidated her, but she was not going to show it. She glared at him defiantly. He had hazel eyes flecked with gold, sparkling fiercely with anger, and an obstinate set to his unshaven jaw.

'No one orders me around,' she defied him. 'I shall check with the police in Xora whether this is a private beach or not.'

For a moment she wondered whether she had gone too far. Had mentioning the police been a mistake? But, to her relief, he took a step away from her.

'As you wish.' He sounded less aggressive now. 'Although I promise you they will tell you the same thing.' Then, his hand on the buckle of his leather belt, he asked almost pleasantly, 'Is the water cold?'

'Why don't you find out for yourself?' Sally replied, unwilling to relax her guard. Was he playing cat and mouse with her?

The American shrugged, apparently amused by her challenging tone. He began to peel off his jeans and she looked quickly away. He came to stand in front of her, grinning at her discomfiture, and she saw he was wearing swimming trunks underneath. 'Remember

4

what I said—don't let me catch you here again.' Then, in three powerful strides forward, he had flung himself into the sea and was swimming strongly away.

Sally picked up her beach bag and stuffed in her towel. Keeping a wary eye on the stranger's head out at sea, she walked across the beach until she stubbed her toe and stumbled over something hard. She looked down to see that she had been tripped up by a canvas shoulder bag causing the contents to spill out. A sketchpad, obviously the property of the stranger, lay at her feet. She saw a beautiful pencil drawing of the Greek countryside, some ancient ruins in the foreground. Perhaps the American was an eccentric artist who wanted to live like a hermit and enjoyed frightening people away? But would an artist have such a muscular, athletic build? And he was far too authoritative and abrasive to be a beach boy or a hippy.

Whoever he was, he had had no right to order her from the beach in that way—for a minute or two back there she had genuinely been afraid. Could there be a spark of truth in what he had said? Sally didn't think so. And what else had that canvas bag of his contained—rocks? What on earth had he wanted with rocks? she wondered as Xora came into view.

*   *   *

5

'Hello, good afternoon, how are you?' called Nicos as Sally walked through his taverna towards the open patio beyond. She greeted him cheerfully, ordered herself a drink, then went outside to join Fiona and Donna, the two other SunSea representatives. They favoured Nicos' taverna because he was friendly and efficient, and because of the splendid view from the vine-shaded patio.

They could either look up, to watch the progress of the bunches of tiny unripe grapes, or out across the village of whitewashed box-like houses sprawling over the hillside, enlivened here and there by startling splashes of purple bougainvillaea and scarlet hibiscus. Below, a rickety, patched wooden jetty, to which a collection of equally rickety and patched fishing boats was moored, stuck out into the sea. Out in the bay a handful of yachts rode at anchor, their fortunate owners sailing between the Greek islands all summer long. In both directions stretched the beautiful sandy beach which, along with the safe bathing in clear waters, the watersports, and the friendliness of the villagers, attracted more and more holidaymakers each year.

But Sally had come to love the nights best, when the sky was sprinkled with stars more brilliant than she had ever seen before, and the scent of jasmine wafted on the breeze.

She caught a trace of its scent now, less

6

strong during the daytime, as she greeted Fiona and Donna and sat down. Nicos bustled up with a tray of tall, ice-cold drinks and a large pastry for Fiona.

'That'll make you fat,' said Donna.

'I know, but I have no willpower where cakes are concerned.' Fiona sighed.

'Join the club,' said Sally, eyes twinkling. Fiona was the youngest of the three, with dark curly hair, a well-rounded figure and a bright bubbly personality. She and Donna had worked in Xora together the previous year, and made a good team. Donna was a couple of years older than Sally, as tall as her, with an enviable figure and rich dark red hair. Her customary expression was distracted, carrying as she did most of the responsibility for the holidaymakers, and because her boy friend Colin was an airline co-pilot and so their time together was snatched and erratic.

'In fact,' said Sally, watching Fiona tuck into her pastry with relish, 'I'm going to weaken right now and have one, too. Swimming always gives me an appetite.'

'So that's where you've been! We wondered where you sloped off to in the afternoons.'

'Which beach do you swim from? Down there?'

'No, way beyond the point. About a mile or two the other way.'

Donna frowned. 'I'm sorry, Sally, I should have told you before, but I didn't think you'd go that far. We aren't supposed to go along there.'

'Why?' Despite the heat of the afternoon, Sally felt cold with surprise.

'I'm not entirely sure, but if you drive along the coast road, inland from there, you'll see plenty of signs forbidding photography. There may be a military camp—the Greeks are very sensitive about those—or perhaps a rusty old hulk left over from the war.'

'I was certainly warned off the beach in no uncertain terms this afternoon—but by an American who was no rusty old hulk.'

'I wonder . . .' Donna began reflectively. 'No, it can't be—they haven't arrived yet. I heard that a film is going to be made here on Kouros, but I shouldn't think he was anything to do with that.'

'Really? What sort of film?' Fiona asked.

'One of those fantasy films with lots of special effects, back in the heroic age with ancient gods and mythological beasts.'

'Sounds very up-to-date,' commented Fiona.

'I think it's all based on Poseidon, the god of the sea. Apparently there was a strong cult of worship for him here about three thousand years ago. Or was it two?'

'The American didn't say anything about a film. In fact, I got the distinct impression that he shouldn't have been there himself.'

'But it's probably best if you don't go there again, just to be on the safe side,' Donna said.

8

'I suppose so—although I'd hate him to think I was taking any notice of *his* warning.'

*   *   *

Nicos brought Sally's pastry, and she began to eat it hungrily. 'By the way,' said Donna, leaning back in her chair. 'Are we all set for tonight's welcoming party? The new arrivals have all settled in, and the returning holiday makers took off safely for England. And don't forget, Sally, tomorrow you're taking the trip on the yacht to Micro Aspro island.'

'I'm looking forward to it. Any last-minute instructions?'

'No, I think we've covered everything. Don't forget to rendezvous with Captain Samuelson about eight-thirty in the morning.'

Sally had only been working in Xora for a few weeks, and had been detailed to conduct a day trip to a nearby island which boasted a small chapel, the ruins of an ancient village and—best of all—a 'blue' grotto.

She left the taverna to return to her room to change. The house was near the centre of the village, in a quiet and shady street. It had its own courtyard at the front, and along one side of the paved yard was a collection of cans, plastic containers and terracotta urns all, in typical Greek fashion, converted into pots for bright red geraniums, pink striped carnations, and herbs.

9

The house belonged to Sofia, a handsome widow who still wore black, although her husband had died many years before. She and Sally nodded to one another in friendly fashion, but as yet the girl didn't feel confident enough of her smattering of Greek to attempt a conversation.

Sofia rented out two rooms at the top of her house. Sally's was the bigger with a scrubbed wooden floor dotted with homemade rugs and an ancient brass bedstead which creaked alarmingly in the night but was very comfortable. There was a bathroom and shower next door, which Sally shared with the occupants of the other room whom she rarely saw.

She considered herself very lucky in her balcony which boasted more pots of scarlet and salmon-pink geraniums, and a view out to sea which she never tired of.

But this afternoon she felt pleasantly drowsy after her long walk, and lay down on the bed to rest a while. She fell immediately into a deep, heavy sleep, as if she had been drugged.

When first she opened her eyes, she couldn't remember where she was. The dim shapes of furniture loomed before her, distorted by darkness; a pale glimmer of light at the window showed that the sun had set. For some unaccountable reason, Sally felt a sense of dread.

Then her vivid dream returned to her, and

10

she shuddered with dread at the thought of it.

She was swimming, and in desperate danger. A shark! The blunt snout of the huge fish had been only inches away, and she had seen its rows of sharp, death-dealing teeth snap dangerously close to her. Then, somehow, in the way of dreams, she was on the shore watching while someone else was being hunted by the shark. As she watched in terror, it closed in on the other swimmer, who seemed as yet unaware of it. She tried to call out, to warn him, but she was frozen in horror and no sound came out.

She tried again and again to call out, but it seemed her whole body was paralysed. Just as its mouth opened for the kill, the swimmer lifted his face from the water and she could see him clearly: it was the American who had ordered her from the beach.

Sally buried her face in her hands. They were coming again, the dreams from which she had sought to escape. She had hoped that completely new surroundings, new people, would free her from them. Admittedly this was a new variant, with a shark and the man from the beach, but yet again she herself had seen danger and been unable to warn anyone of it.

She sat up abruptly, seeking the light switch. Once the room was softly illuminated, the grip of the nightmare receded and she told herself she must put it right out of her mind.

The yowling of cats fighting and scavenging

in the dustbins outside brought her swiftly back to the present. Whatever was she doing sitting here when Donna and Fiona must be waiting for her? It was after seven o'clock and she was already late.

*　　　*　　　*

Within twenty minutes, forgoing her shower and hurrying through the back streets, Sally arrived at the Poseidon Bar. It was bright with lights and lively with voices. She spotted Donna's red hair immediately, and made straight for her.

'Hello, sorry I'm late. I fell asleep,' she apologised breathlessly.

'That's all right. Help yourself to a drink—you look as if you need one.'

'I'm OK. I had a nightmare about a shark, that's all.'

'Speaking of sharks—trouble is on its way,' Donna said, glancing over Sally's shoulder.

Sally looked round and saw with dismay a middle-aged couple bearing down on them through the throng of newcomers enjoying the party. It was Mr. and Mrs. Grundey, only too well-known to Sally. They were both short; Mrs. Grundey with frizzed hair and a flowery dress, Mr. Grundey less broad in the beam and sporting a Hawaiian shirt and a straw pork-pie hat. All ages and types of people travelled with Sun Sea—currently the youngest was six months, the oldest a lively seventy—and each and every one got as much as they could from their holiday.

But the Grundeys had complained about everything from the moment they arrived. Their room was too small and too noisy, their sheets weren't changed often enough, and they seemed convinced the daily maid was a would-be thief, standing guard over her until she finished so that they could lock up after her. The food was too greasy, they couldn't make themselves understood in the shops, and they worried about stinging insects, scorpions and jellyfish. Maybe none of this would have mattered if they hadn't been so unpleasant about it.

Worst of all, the Grundeys had grumbled about Sally, too. Being new and inexperienced, she'd given them cause by misdirecting their luggage on arrival in the village. They'd also muttered unpleasantly when she couldn't find answers to all their questions, even though she'd promised to do her best to find out anything they wanted to know.

Her heart sank as they approached, looking disgruntled as usual. Why were they here?

'Good evening,' she said with a bright smile. 'How are you today?'

'It's been too hot,' Mrs. Grundey complained, fanning herself ineffectually with a small, plump hand.

'That new room you've given us is certainly

13

big enough,' added Mr. Grundey, 'but it's completely airless. We tossed and turned uncomfortably all last night.'

'I'm sorry to hear it. Perhaps if you—'

'That's not why we're here,' interrupted Mrs. Grundey. 'This boat trip tomorrow . . .'

'Please,' Sally prayed, *'don't* let them come.'

'Yes, I'll be conducting it.'

The couple exchanged glances as if to say, 'Oh dear, not *her.*'

'Do we have to pay extra—that's what we want to know?'

'Yes, a thousand drachmas each.'

'But that's daylight robbery!' cried Mrs. Grundey. 'I mean, it's only a sailing boat, isn't it?'

'There are certain expenses to be met—the crew, for example, and free drinks and sandwiches are provided,' Sally replied as calmly as she could. 'If you'd like to sign up, there are two places left.'

'May as well, I suppose. At least it should be cooler on the sea,' Mr. Grundey said unenthusiastically.

'Oh, all right. What time tomorrow, Miss?'

Everyone else called her Sally, but not these two. She said as politely as she could, 'Between eight and eight-thirty. Shall I see you there?' And before they could protest about the early hour, she moved quickly away to concentrate on the new arrivals.

Inside, she was seething. There was always

someone who looked on the black side. It seemed as if they were almost deliberately finding fault. Were they a 'plant' sent by SunSea to test their respresentatives' professionalism? Sally hoped against hope that they would change their minds before morning, for if they came something was sure to go wrong.

*   *   *

It was already bright and hot with a cloudless blue sky when Sally arrived at the harbour the next day. She had slept surprisingly well, and breakfasted on coffee and thick, creamy yogurt and Greek honey, before proceeding to the jetty, clipboard under her arm. Most of the fifteen day trippers were already assembled, including Mr. and Mrs. Grundey.

'Which one is it, then?' asked Charlie, a young Londoner who, with his wife Sadie, was taking a much needed day off from their three small and active children. Sally had arranged a babysitter for them.

'I'm sorry, I don't know,' she confessed, looking at the yachts in the bay and hoping the Grundeys weren't listening. 'I can't read the names from here.'

Charlie swept the bay with his big, expensive binoculars. '*Dolphin*, wasn't it? Then that's the one. A good thirty-footer, and nicely handled.'

Sally and the others admired the graceful

lines of the gleaming yacht Charlie pointed out, which had just hove into view, its sails being trimmed by two indistinct figures.

The young Greek who was to row them to the boat in parties of three or four—the usual powered craft was, for some obscure reason, unavailable—had arrived, and soon everyone was aboard except Sally, the Grundeys and two friends, Marion and Jean, who were first to climb nimbly on deck. Mr. and Mrs. Grundey's progress was slower, and accompanied by pained grunts. Sally settled herself happily in the prow, watching the water ripple past as Takis rowed with a strong and even pull. Looking down, she could see every detail of the weed and rocks on the sea-bed, with glimpses of the sand in between and the occasional flash of colour as a shoal of little fish swam past.

Today was going to be all right, she thought contentedly to herself. The boat bumped against the yacht's hull. Takis caught hold of the wooden ladder and held it steady while Jean and Marion, giggling hysterically, made their way up it. Mrs. Grundey, ascending, found it a much more difficult task.

At last they were all safely ensconced on deck, and it was Sally's turn. She started up just as a high speed motorboat came roaring past in a flurry of spray, pulling two water skiers. The wash rocked both boats and Sally's foot slipped. For one heart-stopping moment

16

she thought she was going to fall.

Then a strong brown hand reached down and firmly gripped her wrist. 'I've got you, you won't fall,' a man's voice said from above, Sally looked up into a circle of smiling faces. 'Thank you,' she said, narrowing her eyes against the sunlight. 'I must have looked pretty silly . . .'

The words died on her lips as she found herself looking straight into the face of the American from the beach.

CHAPTER TWO

'We meet again,' he said as he helped Sally up. Once more she was looking into faintly mocking hazel eyes, almost cat-green in the morning light. The small drama over, the day trippers moved away leaving Sally to face the American alone. She opened her mouth to question him but he intercepted her.

'Dean Samuelson,' he introduced himself, holding out his hand. 'And this is my yacht, the *Dolphin*.'

'Sally Johnson—but you know that already.' His clasp was firm. When he let go, she felt herself sway.

'It's the movement of the boat—you'll get used to it. Unless I'm speaking to an experienced sailor already?'

'No, this is my first time on a yacht. It's very

beautiful.' She looked admiringly at the tall mast, fresh paintwork and gleaming brass.

'Thanks. I'm proud of her myself.' His manner, unlike the first time they had met, was quite courteous.

'Do you need a large crew to sail her?'

'Just one other besides me—my "cabin boy" over there.'

Sally looked round and saw a lad of about sixteen with a shock of tow-coloured hair. He was naked to the waist and wearing ragged cut-off jeans. Although he was busying himself with some ropes, he glanced up as if sensing their eyes upon him—then just as quickly turned his back on them. Sally sensed a cold dislike directed towards her. She tried to dismiss the impression immediately—after all, they'd never met before. He had no reason to take against her.

'Only the two of you?' she said to mask her confusion.

'It's enough. His name is Simon, and he's dumb. I make a point of telling everyone so they don't think he's being rude when he doesn't speak. But he's clever and can communicate when necessary, even if you don't understand sign language.'

'And now,' he went on briskly, 'while you make sure everyone is settled, I'll get the *Dolphin* under way.'

As Sally picked her way around the yacht, checking that each of her charges

18

was comfortable, she was kept too busy to puzzle over young Simon's hostility towards her and the question she longed to ask Dean Samuelson was why had he ordered her off that beach the day before?

The Grundeys had elected to settle down in the cabin.

'You've chosen a good place,' Sally said to them cheerily. 'It's very neat, isn't it?'

Apart from two cushioned benches along either side, with a small table between them, there was no other furniture and no sign of the owner's belongings. But the Grundeys reception of her was chilling and Sally sought out a spot on deck.

Perched on top of the tarpaulin covering of some indistinguishable lumpy object, she watched Dean working closely with Simon to bring up the anchor and set the sails. Then the American took the wheel to guide the *Dolphin* out into deeper waters. There was a stiff breeze and the yacht soon settled into a steady speed, the wind occasionally skimming up a cloud of spray and raining it down on those intrepid enough to be sitting near the prow. When Sally looked back she could see the village of Xora dwindling in size until it blended completely into the dark outline of Kouros island. Then that too dropped out of sight until only the tips of the hills were visible.

*   *   *

They travelled through blue and white—the cerulean blue of the Aegean with its small foam-topped waves, the brilliant blue of the sky framing the white sails. On the horizon an occasional glimpse of a mysterious rocky island shrouded in heat haze put Sally in mind of the days when Ulysses had voyaged these waters which were inspiration indeed for a legend.

A shadow fell across her, interrupting her reverie and she looked up.

'Hi, can I join you?' Dean Samuelson asked.

'Yes, of course.' She shifted aside to make room for him, then a thought struck her. 'Who's—?'

'Simon's guiding the yacht,' he said, guessing her question. Sally glanced across to see Simon fiercely gripping the helm, a look of rapt concentration on his face.

'Has he worked with you a long time?'

'A few months, but he was already a highly experienced sailor. I know his parents and they asked if I could help out by bringing him with me to Greece. He's having emotional difficulties growing up, and they thought he might gain confidence by leaving them and living with me,' he replied.

'And has he?' Sally looked at the boy sympathetically. Because of what had happened to her, she felt she could understand his frustration at not being able to speak.

Dean grinned suddenly and disarmingly,

and Sally's earlier harsh judgment of him was forgotten. 'What do you think? Of course it's done him the world of good.'

'Yes,' she said lightly, 'you've got plenty of confidence so some of it must rub off. You were certainly confident enough to order me off the beach.'

Dean looked away for a second. 'I guess you're not going to let me forget that in a hurry, are you?'

'Not until I find out why, or what it is you've got against me.'

He smiled widely, taking in her golden skin and wide blue eyes. 'I've got nothing against you. Quite the opposite, in fact.'

Sally was disconcerted by his expression and asked in a businesslike tone, 'Did you know who I was yesterday? And wasn't it a mean trick to play, keeping me in the dark like that?'

'I promise you I had no idea who you were at the time, nor that you weren't spinning me a line when you said you worked for SunSea.'

'Meaning,' Sally said sharply, 'that you've checked up on me since?'

'My, you're touchy. Aren't you flattered by my interest?'

Sally was about to retort when she saw the twinkle in Dean's eye and had to grin instead. 'By the way,' she said, 'I learned yesterday that the local police aren't keen on anyone going to that beach and beyond—so how come it's OK for you?'

Dean's reply was, unfortunately, interrupted by a shout from Charlie who had been busy with his binoculars again.

'Look over there—dolphins!'

*   *   *

Excited exclamations resounded all over the boat as everyone craned to see the graceful, joyful animals leaping and diving beside the yacht.

Dean steadied Sally with a hand at her waist as they watched, his body close to hers. For a moment she wanted to lean back and be held close against him. To distract herself, she said, 'Aren't they wonderful? I've never seen them in the wild before. Aren't they supposed to be bringers of good fortune—or is it fair weather?'

'So they say,' he murmured, his lips disturbingly close to her face. 'That makes another first for you today. Perhaps we can make it three?'

She looked into his eyes, and read there the message that, if they'd been alone, he would have tried to kiss her. Would she have let him? She quickly looked away, suddenly feeling all her senses heightened and time stretching so that this moment was out of her normal existence. It seemed they would be travelling forever across the sea with the wind in the sails, dolphins bounding beside them in the water.

Then, in an instant, her dream returned to her and it was as if a cloud had passed across the sun. She twisted round to face him. 'Dean, I must tell you. I had a strange dream about you yesterday—'

His eyebrows rose as he interrupted her. 'Now it's my turn to be flattered.'

'No, listen to me, it was horrible. You were being attacked by a shark and I tried to warn you—'

Dean shook his head dismissively. 'Anxiety, that's all—forget it. But I'm sorry I caused you nightmares. Honey, I must get the wheel,' he said, and in a second had gone.

The wind had suddenly changed direction, catching the bows of the yacht and the *Dolphin* shuddered against it. Then Dean was in control and, almost as if nothing had happened, the yacht was flying smoothly forward. It seemed no one else had noticed the split second of danger.

Sally was glad she had told him about her dream. Now she had voiced her fears, she could see that he was right. It was only her old anxieties playing tricks on her again. She looked across at his tall muscular body, clad in jeans and T-shirt, and smiled to herself. What would her friend Sue have made of Dean Samuelson? After observing his male charms, she would probably have said: 'He's just the kind of distraction you need.'

23

Sally felt a warm burst of affection for her friend. Dear, kind, practical Sue. It was thanks to her she had come to Greece in the first place. Sue worked for a travel agency and, noticing that Sally was becoming thin and pale after the strain of the winter, had given her name to SunSea when one of their regular representatives had had an accident. They were a small local firm in Oxford, and needed a replacement urgently.

'But I don't know the first thing about the travel world,' Sally had protested.

'There are two very experienced people there. You'll learn in no time.'

'And it's Greece, isn't it? I've never been there before. Supposing I can't take the heat?'

'You're just making excuses. It'll be ideal for you—a change of scene is exactly what you need.'

Sally had shaken her head doubtfully.

'What is it you're afraid of?' Sue had asked gently. 'The accident wasn't all that long ago. You deserve a break, something new.'

'I don't know . . . I hate running from my problems, I suppose.'

Sue took her shoulders in a firm grip. 'Sally, all you need is to get a new perspective on things, and then you'll see how silly you've been, to let it weigh on your mind like this. Just think,' she enthused, 'all the sun, sea and sand you could want for a whole summer!'

And so far, she had been proved right . . .

A ripple of conversation among the passengers interrupted Sally's thoughts, and she stood up to stretch her stiff legs. Ahead of them lay a small rocky island. Dean announced that they were approaching Micro Aspro, their destination.

*   *   *

The *Dolphin* was moored at the mouth of a rocky, horse-shoe shaped bay. The tiny beach was encircled by smooth boulders, and at one end two large fig trees provided shade. The only sounds on the barren island were their voices and the shrill of the ubiquitous cicadas.

Sally's party was rowed ashore, and Dean and Simon had returned to the yacht. She issued the plan for their day—a short rest, then a walk across the island to view the grotto, and after that everyone's time was their own until reassembly at the beach just before four. She had just finished outlining the programme when there was a loud splash, followed by scattered applause from the day trippers. She turned round and saw Dean swimming through the crystal clear water of the bay. The clapping had been for his spectacular dive from the deck of the yacht.

'Hi,' he said, casually borrowing Sally's towel to dry himself off. 'Thought I'd come along too, if that's OK?'

Sally nodded. 'Of course. But won't you

25

need some clothes?'

'Charlie brought them over.' And he pointed to a pile on a rock.

But when they left the beach along the dusty path that led across Micro Aspro, Sally found herself trapped beside Mr. and Mrs. Grundey.

'Did you enjoy the boat trip?' she asked.

'I thought it would never end. It seemed almost to tip over several times, and I couldn't see any proper lifeboats neither. I think it's a disgrace,' Mrs. Grundey burst out as she'd obviously been longing to. Mr. Grundey nodded in agreement.

'There's no cause for worry,' Sally reassured them. 'The Captain is a very experienced sailor, and SunSea wouldn't recommend a trip that wasn't completely safe.'

'Huh,' Mr. Grundey snorted. 'Fat lot of use them lifebelts would be if it went down. What about the sharks?'

'There's no sharks in the Mediterranean,' Sally said, repressing a smile. 'At least, not big ones.'

'As for that captain—he's too young to know anything about boats. Irresponsible, too, if you ask me. Leaving that poor mite in charge so he could chat you up. Don't think I didn't see you, because I did,' Mrs. Grundey finished maliciously.

Sally's cheeks burned, but with anger not guilt. Before Mrs. Grundey could continue— Sally could practically hear the words 'And you're no better than you should be' trembling on her lips—she said curtly; 'If you have any complaints, speak to Miss Dawson when we return.'

She dropped back to avoid talking further to them. She knew she had practically invited them to make a complaint, but she didn't care. She could imagine Mrs. Grundey at home, aptly named, forever twitching the net curtains to in outrage. She did not like the idea that she had been spied on, and that Dean Samuelson had been all but accused of incompetence and philandering. Peremptory and strong-willed he might have shown himself to be yesterday, but he was a man to depend on in a crisis, she was sure.

*   *   *

Heat had settled over the tiny island like an invisible cloud. The only noises to break the silence were the sharp buzz of the cicadas calling to one another in the trees and bushes, and the occasional plopping noise of a fish surfacing. It was early afternoon and the sun blazed down from an unblemished sky. Even in the shade, the air was hot and still.

Inland, the island had proved flat and featureless, apart from the ruins of a small Ionian village, but the blue grotto had been an enchanting natural attraction, well worth the visit everyone agreed—although Sally

27

did not solicit the Grundeys' opinion. You didn't have to be a swimmer, either, to reach it. After spending some time photographing and sightseeing, the day trippers split up and spread out across the island. Dean melted away at that point, and Sally did not know where he had gone.

She wandered back to their arrival point with Charlie and Sadie where they swam and afterwards shared a picnic and a bottle of retsina. Then sleep claimed them all.

Sally awoke, her face stinging from its proximity to the sand. The sun was burning her feet which now protruded from the fig tree's enveloping shade. She sat up and brushed the sand from her clothes, then leaned forward, clasping her hands around her knees. A few feet away her companions were still asleep, Sadie's head resting on her husband's chest and his arm protectively around her shoulders. Their easy show of affection tugged at Sally's heart. She wasn't usually prone to feeling loneliness. There had been boy friends before, but nothing serious. She hadn't felt ready to become deeply involved.

She heard a noise behind her and saw Dean scrambling down to the beach. He waved, and she stood up to join him.

'Have you been exploring the island?' she asked.

'Not much to see, but I had a look around the ruined village, and a quick dip in the sea.

Did you look at the village?'

Sally shook her head. 'I've been lazing here with Charlie and Sadie.'

'You're more interested in acquiring a suntan than looking at antiquities. Some people prefer to spend all their time doing just that—not that it's necessarily a good idea, but you're missing out if you don't take advantage of your stay here to look around.'

Sally shook her head decisively. 'I've noticed, and no doubt they enjoy it enormously, but not me. I really can't understand how people can get so excited about ancient chunks of stone.'

'But isn't it exciting to find out how human beings used to live?'

'No, I don't think so. There are so many more important things happening now. I think they should teach us about the future and space and technology at school, not musty old bits of wood.'

Dean frowned. 'You're being rather narrow-minded, Sally. The past can tell us all sorts of things about ourselves, the Greek philosophers in particular. Things that can help our present and our future.'

'How can knowing how flour was ground in 3000 BC, or that they once tossed spears at sabre-toothed tigers, have any relevance to today?' Sally warmed to the argument, disgruntled because she felt that Dean had disapproved of her lack of interest in

29

antiquities, and had been reproving her. She would not back down now. She was partly disturbed, too, by the thought that her own past might be considered relevant to the present. Wasn't it possible to make a fresh start?

'You've chosen two very extreme examples there, haven't you?' Dean was saying. 'They're just tiny details, specks of colour in the complete portrait. When you look at the whole thing, then it does start to make sense.'

Sally suddenly remembered Dean's sketchpad, and realised why he was defending ancient history. 'I'm sorry,' she said. 'I know you like to draw pictures of old ruins and things, so obviously you like them. But you can't expect me to, as well. We're all made differently.'

Dean stared at her. 'How did you know that—about my drawing?' he asked. Although his voice was casual, Sally sensed that her answer was important to him.

'I stubbed my toe on your bag yesterday— you'd left it lying on the beach. Which conveniently brings us back to the question you've managed to avoid answering so far— why were you trying to frighten me away, and how is it OK for you to be there?'

Dean hesitated for a moment then spread his hands in a conciliatory gesture. 'You could say I own it.'

'Oh!' Sally gave a rueful smile. Of course.

If he owned his own yacht, why not a Greek beach? 'Well, why didn't you say so in the first place?'

'I guess I didn't want the word to get around too quickly. I'm not the only one who's been after that area of land, you see.'

She nodded. 'Did you think someone would try to stop you—from owning it, I mean? It's difficult for foreigners to buy land here in Greece, isn't it?'

Dean nodded. 'Very. It's taken me—'

'Hi there, you two. Is it time to leave already?' Sadie called out, woken by the sound of their voices.

'Hi,' Sally called out and turned to walk towards her, but Dean had taken hold of her arm.

'Here,' he said, digging in his jeans pocket. 'I picked this up for you, but I guess you won't want it now, judging from your hatred of everything that's more than five minutes old.'

'What is it?' Sally asked curiously.

'Just something I found in the water when I was swimming. I thought you might like it as a souvenir of our trip today.'

He placed the hard object in her hand. It was warm from being close to his flesh, and Sally looked down at it carefully.

'It seems to be some kind of coin,' she said. 'Or a medallion.'

Dean shrugged. 'I suppose so. For all I know it could have been dropped by the last

31

set of tourists on Micro Aspro.'

While Sally turned the object over in her palm, Dean looked at his watch. 'Should be getting off soon. I think I'll head back for the *Dolphin* now and wake Simon up. It always takes him at least quarter of an hour to come to after a nap.'

'Thanks for the souvenir, Dean. I'll remember today—'

'Your day of firsts—but we've yet to make it three.'

Before Sally could say anything more, he was heading across the beach. She examined his gift again. It seemed too big to be a coin. One side was almost rubbed smooth, but on the other was a clear outline of a bearded head, deepset eyes and thick, curling hair. It looked like a representation of the god Poseidon to Sally, but she wasn't sure. If it was very old it might be valuable, she supposed, and wondered if Dean realised it. But now that he had given it to her as a present, she could hardly give it back.

Some of the other trippers had now arrived back at the beach and Sally slid the medallion into her bag, pleased that Dean had thought of her. He had also been more forthcoming about his mysterious behaviour of the day before. If he was very rich, she wondered if he wanted to keep his new land a secret to throw newspapers off the scent. Quite a few millionaires and film stars had found hideaways in the Greek islands, she knew. But if that was the case, why was he running day trips for SunSea?

She shook her head, puzzled, as she made for the new arrivals. Dean had only to answer one question for five more to rear their ugly heads!

*   *   *

The return journey to Xora was a quiet one, with most of the passengers sleepy from the sun. The Grundeys had taken the cabin again—looking very put out when another, younger couple joined them in there—and Sally gave them a wide berth.

All too soon the outline of Kouros lay before them on the horizon, bathed in the slanting rays of the afternoon sun. Then they could see *their* village, Xora, gradually getting bigger and bigger until they could make out the houses and inhabitants. It felt to Sally as if she had been away a lot longer than a few hours. While Xora had followed its daily, uneventful rhythm, much had happened to her.

The passengers climbed down into the rowing boat which would take them across to the jetty. Simon lounged against the cabin doorway, his face sullen.

Dean approached Sally. 'Did you enjoy the trip?' he asked.

'Yes, very much—just one thing, though. I hope I'm right and you're a secret millionaire or film star, because if you rely on these trips for your income, we might be running into trouble.' She had decided to tell him about the Grundeys.

When she had finished, he grinned. 'Some people!' he said. 'Let's hope they'll have forgotten all about it when they get home, and will remember only the good times.'

'I don't think they've had any yet!'

'Well, don't worry about me—I do these trips for fun and for a favour, not for cash.' He was about to hand her down the ladder but paused. 'And you'd be doing me a favour if you don't mention my beach to anyone—OK?'

Sally nodded. 'OK. I did mention it to Fiona and Donna, but they don't know the man I met is you.'

Dean blew her a kiss when she had reached the safety of the waiting boat, but was it just a bribe for her to keep her mouth shut about his beach?

CHAPTER THREE

Sally crossed to the window and folded back the shutters. Heat immediately enveloped her body and the brightness of the sun made her blink. Something about the stark, primitive beauty of the scene drew her out on to the balcony so that she could glance over the terracotta red of roofs, the blank whiteness of walls, small lemon trees and shading vines and the wide expanse of blue sea beyond.

It was half-past seven, and Xora had already been awake for some time, for the leisurely village days followed the dictates of the sun. Once it had risen, barely piercing the early morning chill, the first risers stirred. Housewives in slippers and bent old ladies in black whose wrinkled faces were a testament to a life of hardship, converged on the main water tap with buckets and bowls. In the background donkeys brayed, competition for the cockerel's cracked cry.

When the sun had begun to warm the air, the shutters on shops, cafés and tavernas were rattled back, goods were carried out for display and the first batch of loaves was placed in the heated ovens at the bakery. Early morning greetings, as old as recorded time, were exchanged.

Everyone moved slowly as the day heated up. At siesta-time, shutters were closed again against the glare but doors remained open to catch the slightest breeze. Old men dozed on doorsteps, dogs sprawled in the shade, and only the slap, slap of the tourists' sandals on the village's cobblestones disturbed the tranquillity of the narrow streets.

But when the sun began to slide in the sky,

the village came back to life. Voices rose in volume, swelled by those returning from the beach, and a sense of expectancy began to pervade the evening air, along with the more obvious scents of flowers and the tang of slowly barbecuing chicken and lamb basted with oil and rosemary. The streets filled with people eager to see and be seen, for who knows what the night might bring?

Sally knew that this day and evening would bring a lot of hard work for her. It was Wednesday again, when the Sun Sea couriers said goodbye to happy, relaxed holidaymakers headed for home, and welcomed newcomers, pale and excited, from England. During the day the cleaning of rooms and villas had to be supervised, baskets of food and other essential items placed in each apartment, and the airport contacted about flight arrangements.

As the group of homeward-bound travellers waited quietly in the main square, news came that the coach driver was ill. After a great deal of gesticulation and negotiation, Donna traced a replacement but he had to be fetched from his house on the other side of the village.

Sally was instructed to sit by the phone in the office and monitor the airport. The new arrivals would have to wait until the coach arrived, and as for those departing . . . Anxious minutes ticked by until Sally discovered that an air traffic controllers' strike in England had delayed the outward bound flight by nearly two hours. Which was just as well—the new driver refusing to have anything to do with the usual coach.

'Too dangerous,' he decreed for some dark reason of his own, and those leaving had to take a minibus and hastily hired taxis.

'It's *them*, I know it is,' Sally thought to herself. 'They're cursed.' For the Grundeys were leaving too, and yet everything conspired to delay the moment when they would actually leave Greece and Sally could breathe a sigh of relief.

By late afternoon her arm ached from holding the telephone, her head was splitting from having to speak in broken English, and her stomach rumbled from missing lunch. When Donna came into the office, she gave Sally a sympathetic look.

'Come on, let's go and have a drink together—what about my place? Fiona's taking care of everything else for now.'

*   *   *

The house where Donna lived was close to the centre of the village. It was old with its own private walled courtyard. Sally sat outside while Donna went to fetch some drinks.

It was peaceful sitting there under the gently swaying pale green leaves of an oleander bush, watching the pattern of shadows they made on the clean flagstones. A thin, dusty cat lay in the flowerbed, washing its paws, its eyes green slits of pleasure. Sally slowly began to unwind.

Donna brought a plate of black olives, feta cheese and tomatoes for them to eat with some fresh bread, and opened a chilled bottle of wine. She pushed her long, thick red hair back over her shoulders and told Sally to start.

'Thanks, I'm starving.'

'You've worked hard today, and you've worked well since you arrived, but I have some bad news for you. The last thing Mrs. Grundey said to me was that she was going to complain about you.'

Sally sighed and lost her appetite. 'Well, I guessed that was coming. I couldn't seem to do a thing right for them. But it was as if they were looking for trouble at the same time.'

'I shouldn't think it will come to anything. After all you are new, and it would take more than one complaint—even assuming they carry it through—to affect your job,' Donna reassured her. 'And I'll put everything you want to say about them down in writing, too.'

'Thanks. I've been enjoying the job so much that I'd hate to lose it.'

'I'd hate to lose you, too. It's your first job in the travel trade, isn't it? I've not really had a chance to ask you before, we've been so busy these past few weeks.'

'That's right.' Sally continued to eat, aware that Donna was waiting for her to say more.

'What did you do before?'

'I had my own shop—a small boutique—and I used to sell some of my own designs, too. It was successful enough to make a living, just. But I wanted a change, so when this job came up it seemed the answer.' It was not the entire truth, but it wasn't an outright lie either, and her answer seemed to satisfy Donna, who asked her more questions about the kind of clothes she used to sell.

'You were lucky the Grundeys never managed to track down your shop,' she finished, succeeding in bringing a smile to Sally's face.

In fact, Sally was glad to find that it was no longer painful to talk about her old life. What she hadn't told Donna was quite how much she had staked on this new job, having sold up her business.

'Was Dean Samuelson "chatting you up", as Mrs. Grundey put it?' Donna asked next. 'Not that it's any of my business, but she claimed he was endangering people's lives by doing so.'

Sally flushed. 'No—it was nothing more than polite conversation. He put his hand on my back to steady me at one point, that's all. I mean, he was being pleasant but not excessively so. It was just her suspicious mind at work.'

'That's what I thought. From what I've seen of Dean Samuelson, I wouldn't have put him down as a cheap Lothario. Do you like him?'

Sally considered the question. Her feelings

were too complex to describe in terms of like or dislike. 'He seems to me to be a very good sailor,' she said carefully. 'Although I don't know what else he does. And, yes, I do like him.'

'If you ask me, he doesn't need to do anything else. He's just one of the idle rich.'

'That's the impression I got.' It was on the tip of her tongue to tell Donna about his owning the beach, but he had asked her not to. 'Why does he work for SunSea? He mentioned something about it being a favour.'

'Yes, it is. He knows the owner of SunSea, apparently, and when they met up earlier in the year this little arrangement was conceived. It's a good idea, too, a very popular trip.

'We've just got time for some coffee,' Donna continued. 'I'll go and make it now.'

When she returned, she found Sally subdued. 'What's the matter—are you worrying about that complaint? I promise you, it'll be nothing.'

'I don't like to think that I'm doing my job badly.'

'Nonsense,' Donna said firmly. 'Tell you what, let's do something different tonight. How about the disco? We could go along after the drinks party. It never gets going till after ten anyway. It's great fun, and it'll do us both good to have a break. You'll see everything in perspective tomorrow.'

Sally agreed. She had been finding some of

the evenings overlong, when Donna and Fiona were occupied with their own affairs, and sometimes felt rather too much 'the new girl'. She went back to her room to change, while Donna went in search of Fiona to see if she wanted to come too.

As she showered and changed into a red skirt and matching cotton shirt, Sally thought over her conversation with Donna. Had she revealed too much about herself? Donna might well be wondering why she had thrown up her own business to become a travel courier. And if she asked, Sally was not sure she wanted to tell her all about it.

As for the Grundeys, that was a blow. She hoped Donna and Dean Samuelson were right, and that it would come to nothing. And where did Dean get to when he wasn't sailing on the *Dolphin*? She was fairly certain he didn't yet have a house on the land he'd bought, yet she hadn't seen him for a whole week since the trip. It was fortunate for him that today was the closest she'd come to blurting out his secret. Neither Donna nor Fiona had asked her about the 'strange American' again.

Sally combed her hair, pleased with the contrast between its silvery shade and her deep tan. She took out her jewellery box and tipped out the contents, intending to pick out a necklace and earrings. But in the middle of the pile was the medallion Dean had given her, and which she had placed among her other valuables.

She paused to pick it up, running her fingers over the smooth side then the relief of the man's. She shook her head. What a strange man Dean was, full of contradictions, and yet she sensed that there was a rock steady core to him, a deep sense of purpose. She blinked and put the keepsake down. She hoped she could rely on her instincts—they'd let her down in the past, and she very much wanted to be right about Dean.

She picked out a pale pink shell necklace with matching earrings and put them on, then scooped the rest of her jewellery back into the box, all except the old medallion. She left that on the dressing-table, intending to have a hole drilled through it so that she could hang it on a chain.

As she strolled through the village streets towards the Poseidon Bar, where she would introduce herself to the new arrivals, she drank in the sights and sounds around her. She knew now that she loved the village, and loved Greece. She very much hoped she would not have to leave if the Grundeys pushed their case.

*　　　*　　　*

The music at the disco was loud and lively, coloured lights pulsing in time to the rhythm. It was early yet, and only a few people, a mixture of holidaymakers and locals, were at the bar or on the dance floor. This was a paved area open to the sky, unlike any other disco she had seen.

She, Donna and Fiona found themselves a place to sit on a bench under the trees that bounded the dancing area. As Donna had predicted, the upset of the day receded and Sally began to enjoy herself. The three SunSea reps danced and talked together happily until Sally found herself alone when Donna went to the bar to buy drinks and Fiona headed for the Ladies Room.

Sally was watching the dancers when she became aware that she was being watched. She glanced up and saw a man observing her closely. He was on his own, and when he saw that he had attracted her attention, he came over.

'Excuse me for staring at you,' he said politely, 'but I think I know you. You are English, aren't you? My name's Peter Elsing.'

Sally wondered why he was using such a very unoriginal line.

'I'm sure I don't know you,' she replied guardedly. 'I've only recently come out from England anyway.'

'But you lived in Oxford, isn't that right?'

'Yes, but how did you—'

'I knew I was right,' he said triumphantly, sitting down beside her. 'I lived there, too. I lecture in Ancient History at the University.

43

Now, if I remember right, your name is Sally, isn't it?'

'That's right,' she said cautiously. Had he overheard one of the others saying her name or did he really know her?

'You're very distinctive, with that silver hair. You were pointed out to me once—I believe you know the Readings?'

Sally nodded. Sonia Reading always made a point of buying Sally's own designs, and she had been invited to several of their parties. He must have seen her there.

'I hope you don't mind my butting in like this,' Peter Elsing went on, 'but I've spent the last few weeks largely on my own and it's a pleasant surprise to see a familiar face.'

'Are you taking a long holiday?'

'No, I've been luckier than that. A film is to be made, partly here on Kouros, and I'm one of the technical advisers because of my subject.'

'Oh, yes, we've heard about it. It's a mixture of fact and fantasy, isn't it? Has everybody not arrived then?'

'Only me so far. I've been spying out the land, looking for potential locations and picking up information—I even get paid for it!'

'Sounds interesting. Have you been successful?'

'So far, yes. Have you had a chance to look around the island yourself yet?'

'No, I've hardly been out of the village—just

one day trip,' she confessed.

'You could always accompany me, if you wanted. A bargain package—guide and companion in one?'

Sally bit her lip. Peter Elsing, dark and lean, seemed a pleasant enough man, but she felt wary of him.

'I'm at work most of the time,' she told him. 'I'll think about it, but I'm not very interested in old ruins.'

'At work?' He seemed surprised. 'I didn't realise. I thought you—'

*   *   *

He broke off as someone stopped in front of them. It was Dean Samuelson. Sally felt her heart lift and could not prevent a foolish grin from spreading across her face.

'Hi, Sally,' he said easily, although he was looking at Peter Elsing with an impenetrable expression.

'Hello, Dean. Have you met Peter Elsing? He's working on that film which is to be made here.'

'Yes, I've heard something about it. How's it going?'

'Oh, fine,' said Peter. 'It's quite an interesting little island, if you know what you're looking for.'

'I guess so. Well, I've found what I'm looking for.' He smiled down at Sally and held

45

out his hand. 'Want to dance?'

She took his hand and stood up. Peter Elsing stood, too.

'It was nice to talk to you, Sally—and don't forget my offer if you're free.'

'I won't. 'Bye.'

As they began to dance together, Sally waited for Dean to speak first. She had the distinct impression that he had wanted to drive Peter Elsing away but she wasn't entirely sure why.

'Known him long?' Dean asked casually.

'Who, Peter? No—about ten minutes. Although apparently we have mutual friends back home. That's how he recognised me.'

'And what exactly was the nature of his "offer"?'

'To show me the sights of Kouros—why?'

'I'm naturally suspicious where strangers are concerned, I guess.'

'I'd noticed,' Sally remarked drily. 'But to me you're still virtually a stranger, you know.'

'Really—and I thought we were getting on so well. Maybe I'm a little angry that you'd take up his offer when you told me you hated anything more than a year old.'

Sally managed to keep a straight face as she replied, 'I haven't said yes yet. And maybe I've changed my mind in the last week. It's a long time since we argued, and Greece is working its magic on me.'

'Ah, so that's what's bugging you—I haven't

been around for a week. Never mind, we'll just have to make up for lost time now.' He grabbed her round the waist and whirled her round until she was nearly dizzy.

Sally found that dancing close to Dean, feeling his arms around her, was too pleasurable to let her continue the disagreement. But when the music stopped, she said, 'What makes you think I've been pining for you all week? Isn't that called arrogance?'

She had to wait for her answer. The music changed in tempo to a slow, dreamy song and Dean drew her gently into his arms, holding her so that her head rested softly against his shoulder. Then she heard him say, 'Perhaps because I've been thinking of you, I hoped you were thinking of me.'

Sally lifted her head and looked at him. 'Did you really come here to find me, or was it an accident?'

He gave an enigmatic smile. 'A little of both. I had to come here tonight, and I hoped you'd be here. But I didn't expect you to have an admirer in tow already.'

'Peter's not an admirer—he said he was lonely, waiting for the film people to arrive.'

Dean tightened his arms around her. 'Tell you what, I'll make a counter-offer. I'll show you the sights of Kouros, and I can promise you more of an adventure than Elsing could give you. What do you say?'

47

'I'll think about it . . . oh!'

Dean had skilfully danced them away from the lights and other people, and now they were alone, private with only the night sky studded with stars and the silver light of the waning moon to see them. Dean drew Sally even closer to him, and she gladly tightened her arms around him. His face was lit by moonlight, his eyes dark and unfathomable. He kissed her firmly, his mouth practised and sure.

'I shall continue this torture until you say yes,' he announced solemnly.

'In that case—I'm still thinking about it.'

*   *   *

It was after midnight when she entered her room. She was tired but very happy. After Dean had kissed her again, Fiona and Donna had found them and dragged them back on to the dance floor where all four of them had danced energetically till late. They had laughed together, talked of nothing in particular, and Sally felt completely carefree.

She took off her jewellery, then studied her face in the mirror for a long moment as if it could reveal the answer she sought. It had been a magical night, and she closed her eyes as she relived Dean's kisses. She hoped he hadn't only been spurred into action by the sight of Peter Elsing—but then, did it matter what the catalyst was?

She opened her eyes again and began to take off her make-up. Then another thought struck her. Perhaps Mrs. Grundey hadn't been far off the mark when she had accused Dean of trying to 'chat her up'. Perhaps the older woman had sensed something between them before they themselves did? Sally grinned. Poor Mrs. Grundey. She must have her reasons for being so sour—it was just a pity she had had to take it out on Sally.

As she reached for her jewellery box, Sally noticed that something was missing. The medallion she had left on her dressing-table had gone. She was sure she had left it there, ready to take to a jeweller's. She looked in her box, then began to search the floor in case she had dislodged it by mistake. She even picked up the lamp and pushed the bed aside to examine the floor more closely, but it was definitely not there. There were no cracks in the floorboards where it could have rolled through. Perhaps Sofia had been in to tidy up? It was unlikely, though, as she usually did that first thing in the morning.

Sally sighed. It wasn't very important, but it was a shame to have lost Dean's gift so carelessly. She would have another look for it in daylight, then try to forget about it.

She pulled open the top drawer of her chest to put her jewellery box away, then frowned. Surely she hadn't left her T-shirts all screwed up like that? She began to fold them more neatly when another thought struck her. Hadn't the light been on in the room when she'd come in? She was sure she'd left it off when she went out. It hadn't struck her at the time, she'd been too preoccupied thinking about the evening.

Quickly she checked her passport, money and camera, but they were all safe. The only thing that was missing was the medallion. Someone had been in her room and looked through her things; she could be glad that only one thing was missing. Perhaps the intruder had been disturbed and had run off before looking further.

Nevertheless, to be on the safe side, she put a chair under the handle of the door before she got into bed that night.

CHAPTER FOUR

'If you look to your left,' Sally called down the coach, 'you will be able to see the mountain village of Pale Castritsa—that means "ancient castle". The village can only be reached by donkey or on foot, up that zig-zag path there. It was fortified by the Knights of St. John in the twelfth century and from there they were able to keep a sharp look out for Turkish invaders.'

The coach passengers dutifully looked to their left, exclaiming and pointing.

'We'll arrive in Theopolis in about fifteen minutes,' she said once they had had time to look. 'There will be time to stretch our legs and have a drink before setting off for the museum. Afterwards we'll explore the old part of town and have lunch.'

She sat down again in her seat behind the driver and gazed out at the passing landscape. This was the first time she had been back to Theopolis, the capital of Kouros, since she had arrived. It felt odd, after being tucked away in tiny Xora for a month, to be re-entering civilisation again. She had almost forgotten what the hustle and bustle of a busy town was like.

It was two days since the night of the discotheque. She had arranged to meet Dean on Sunday, and found that she was looking forward to seeing him again very much. She also speculated on how he had become one of the 'idle rich', as Donna had called him.

She had asked Sofia if she had seen the missing medallion, and was not surprised when the answer was no. She had wondered whether it was worth telling anyone about the loss, but as she had no real evidence that her room had been entered, she decided against it, although she took extra precautions. The tooting of the coach's horn brought her back to the present with a start. They had entered the outskirts of Theopolis and were driving smoothly along wide avenues lined with trees. Low white houses were set in neat gardens of roses, geraniums and bright scarlet hibiscus.

Soon they came to the town centre. Traffic roared around them, the pavements and cafés were thronged with people, and the coach driver worked hard with brake and horn to force a passage through.

At last he swung into a large coach park right on the waterfront. Tables and chairs from cafés and tavernas spilled from under striped canvas awnings and the harbour was filled with boats. Old Greek fishing *caiques* and sparkling modern yachts bobbed side by side on the calm waters, while a big, inter-island ferry slowly entered the harbour, its rails thronged with people. Sally wondered fleetingly if Dean kept the *Dolphin* here.

She stood up and raised her voice to announce, 'Right everybody, we're here. We'll have a drink and rendezvous in that café over there, the one with the red awning.' There was a general hubbub as people gathered their belongings, and several children ran down the aisle, eager to be first off the coach. 'Be careful,' she warned. 'The water's deep here.'

The museum was housed in a one-storey building of modern construction up a quiet side street. There were several well-lit rooms with display cases containing ancient Greek artefacts—vases, coins and statuettes—and one big room containing reconstructions of temple friezes and two big statues, one of Apollo, the sun god, the other Poseidon, god of the sea. Sally toured the rooms quickly, expecting to be bored. But she found Poseidon, with his sightless eyes and long curled beard, quite awesome.

*   *   *

She stepped outside into brilliant sunshine, and saw that the museum was sited beside a field where some ancient houses were being excavated. She wandered down old pathways, peered into large urns, and inspected the crumbling foundations of villas. It was quite a different feeling from looking at things behind glass, and Sally discovered that she was actually enjoying herself.

The remnants of one villa were nearly complete in layout, its mosaic floors still intact. Sally lingered over these, gazing down at the pattern of stones covered with a fine layer of dust, thinking of the people who had walked there once so many thousands of years ago.

'Barry, if I've told you once I've told you a hundred times—come off them tiles,' admonished an exasperated mother, grabbing her child by the arm. She met Sally's eyes apologetically. 'He's such a good boy usually,' she explained while Barry retorted defensively, 'I was only *playing*, Mum. It's boring here.'

Sally smiled. She knew how he felt, although lately, she had to admit, she was changing her mind. 'Come along, Barry, let's go inside and look at some of those weapons in there. I bet we'll be able to think of some good stories.' She took him by the hand and, as they went indoors, scoured her brain for the bloodthirstiest tales she could remember about the ancient Greek heroes and the battles they had fought.

As they moved among the glass cases, both making an extra effort to be interested, Sally reading the English translations about the contents, something suddenly caught her eye: facsimiles of the coin that Dean had given her, which had disappeared or been stolen. There were several of them, of varying sizes, and incised or stamped on each one was the same design of a head.

'Miss, miss, what is it?'

Barry's small hand tugging at her own brought Sally back to the present.

'It says here: "The people of Kouros Island in ancient times worshipped the God of the Sea, and developed their own cult around him. His image was used on their coins, in various carvings, and the priests used his mask for their rituals".'

'What's "rituals"?' Barry asked.

'Well, sort of prayers and worship,' she replied absent-mindedly, while wondering if Dean had known the coin he'd so carelessly given her was probably very valuable, just as she'd thought at the time.

'Well, I think it's *boring*,' said Barry.

'You're right,' Sally agreed. 'Let's see what the time is—goodness, time to find your mum. We want to look round the shops before lunch.'

She ignored Barry's groans at the mention of shops and began to shepherd her group together for the next part of their outing. The old part of Theopolis was a maze of alleyways and narrow streets where cars were not allowed. Buildings and awnings arched overhead, and it was full of fascinating tiny shops, market stalls and coffee houses. Sally would have liked to spend all day there, browsing over the carpets and blankets, tooled leatherware, brass ornaments of every kind, pretty cotton dresses, carved wooden trinkets, silver jewellery and ceramics—the variety was endless.

What intrigued her, though, was that now that she had seen the coins in the museum she saw the same design everywhere: on plates, tiles, wooden carvings. She would have to tell Dean about it. There might be more where he had found the first one.

The restaurant where they ate lunch was packed and noisy. Its decor was unpretentious, huge fans circling creakily on the ceiling, walls were decorated with thousands of yellowing postcards from all over the world. But the food, mainly fish, was delicious. Sally, seated between two very friendly couples, was soon engaged in lively conversation with them, and put the mystery of the coin to the back of her mind for now.

* * *

Dean and Sally had arranged to meet outside a café after breakfast on Sunday. He had said he would 'hire some transport', but Sally had not expected him to turn up on a powerful Suzuki motorbike. Immediately all her pleasure at seeing him drained away, and she sat rooted to her chair. He parked it on its stand, looked at it admiringly, then came over to kiss her casually on the cheek.

He froze as he saw the expression on her face.

'What's the matter? Has something happened?' he asked with concern.

'No, I—I didn't expect you to bring a motorbike, that's all.' 'All!' her mind echoed. 'If only he knew . . .'

'Haven't you ridden one before? It's perfectly safe, especially in the hands of someone like me. That's not idle boasting either. I've done some stunt riding in my time.'

Slowly Sally stood up. 'It's not that. I'm sure you're very good. It's just—you do see a lot of accidents here.'

'That's because all kinds of people hire

56

mopeds who've never ridden before, or who haven't used a bike in years. It's much better than a stuffy motor car in this heat, don't you think?'

Sally allowed him to lead her over to the gleaming machine, then stopped. 'It's a long time since I've ridden pillion. I expect I'll be a little nervous.'

'In that case, shut your eyes and hold on to me.' Dean smiled, but he saw his words were not having the reassuring effect he had hoped. 'Hey, Sally, you can trust me,' he said, putting a finger under her chin and looking into her eyes. 'But if you're really worried, I can easily change it for a car.'

Sally hesitated. It was indeed a challenge. She could carry on living in fear—she could take it up and declare the past well and truly conquered.

'It's OK. We'll take the bike.'

'Fine. I promise I'll take it easy, no daredevil tricks, I promise you. Now, where would you like to go?'

'I don't have the first idea. Can you suggest somewhere?'

'I was hoping you'd say that. We'll take the main road across the interior, cool off at one of the little villages on the other side, then I'll take you somewhere special for lunch.'

'Sounds great.' She eyed the bike nervously. 'Well, I suppose we'd better get it over with.'

Dean put his arm around her shoulder and

gave her a brief squeeze. 'Don't make it sound like a trip to the dentist. You'll see—you'll love it.'

He kicked the machine into life and they cruised slowly out of the village until they came on to the main highway.

'You OK back there?'

'I think so,' Sally called back, her stomach churning and her palms cold with apprehension.

'Take hold then—here we go.'

Sally clasped her arms around his waist and leaned against his broad back. He was wearing a short-sleeved, brightly coloured shirt, and she could see the muscles in his arms stand out as he gripped the handlebars. As usual he wore jeans, and Sally was glad that she had opted for dungarees and a T-shirt. As the bike roared beneath her, she closed her eyes, and remembered.

*   *   *

She had known Paul for years. He was a good friend, and they often went around together, or spent hours talking about their boy or girl friend troubles. Paul had had a motorbike, much like this one, and he had been very proud of it, spending hours stripping its engine and polishing the chrome. He had taken Sally for quite a few spins on it, and she had enjoyed the feeling of freedom as they had whizzed

58

through the country lanes of Oxfordshire, the wind whipping colour into their cheeks.

Paul had given her a lift to the party that night, in the autumn of last year. He had told her that he had fallen in love, and was hoping that the girl would be at the party too. She was—with someone else. Paul had been very upset, and had drunk far too much.

Eventually Sally decided that she would ring for a taxi, and went to tell Paul, sitting morosely in a corner, that it would arrive in ten minutes. He had immediately jumped up and told her off for interfering. 'I'm perfectly all right,' he'd said in a too-loud voice as he pushed her aside. 'I'm going on my bike.'

She'd tried to hold him back, she'd even asked others to help, but the party was nearing its end and not everyone understood what was happening. After Paul had driven off into the darkness, narrowly missing the gatepost, she'd waited in agony for the taxi to arrive, and asked the driver to follow the same route he would take.

It was too late by the time they arrived. He'd skidded on a bend where the road was wet, and had gone head first into a brick wall.

Although Sally knew she'd done all she could to stop him, she couldn't help feeling guilty; that she might somehow have saved him and had failed to. The dream she had had after first meeting Dean had been like that. She knew she only had to call out and he would be saved, yet she could not. She had failed.

Sally opened her eyes and gazed dry-eyed into the distance. She had finished her grieving for Paul, and could think of him now with affectionate warmth. If only she could lose the feeling of failure so easily. Her friend Sue had hoped that coming to Greece would help but as yet Sally knew she was not entirely free of the past.

The dry dusty landscape slipped by them as the road climbed between fields of low-lying vines, with an occasional glimpse of a single-storey white house surrounded by a garden of colourful flowers. Once they passed a whole field of golden sunflowers, all facing the sun. All the time they were making their way towards the dark, rugged slopes of the distant mountains.

As the Suzuki ate up the miles they met little traffic, bar one or two cars, an elderly Greek bus piled high with luggage and mysterious parcels tied in black plastic on top, and then a flock of goats. Dean stopped to let them by, their bells tinkling in the still air. Sally's ears hummed in the silence after the rush of wind and the roar of the bike's powerful engine.

*　　　*　　　*

Although the road skirted the wilder parts of the mountains, Sally felt they were leaving the inhabited parts behind.

Then, the road dropped away and ahead she could see the sea, stretching clear and empty to the horizon, while below a village sat amid tall cypruses and silver-leaved olive trees.

They parked by a scrubby tree in a small, dusty square, and a few small boys ran forward to examine the motor bike. There was a single café. Men dressed in dark, sombre clothes sat outside at tables, clicking worry beads through their fingers, watching Dean and Sally expressionlessly from under peaked caps.

'Fancy a drink?' said Dean, and Sally nodded although she felt the men were hostile. But when they went over, they were met with shy smiles, and two men immediately moved to allow them a table to themselves. Along with their thick, sweet coffee a shallow dish of nuts and sunflower seeds was brought for them to eat.

'This is well off the tourist track, isn't it?' said Sally. 'I'm glad we came here. It has a lovely atmosphere.'

'Not a souvenir shop in sight,' Dean agreed. 'And those donkeys over there are about the fastest form of transport.'

Sally drank some of her coffee, and felt herself beginning to relax. She hadn't realised how tense she had been while they were driving along.

'Did you enjoy the ride?' asked Dean. 'You acted like an experienced passenger—perhaps you've had an accident, is that it?'

'Not me, a friend of mine. I haven't been on a bike since, until today.'

Dean grinned. 'Another first. I'm collecting them. Do you want to tell me about it?'

Sally began to talk, slowly at first, then expanding on her story as she felt she'd like to tell Dean everything. Then, to her horror, she realised that he was barely listening.

'Sally, time's getting on. We'd better make tracks now, OK?'

He tossed some coins on to the table, waved to the café proprietor, then strode quickly to the motorbike. Sally followed, hurt that he had not been interested in her tale, after all. Perhaps she had been mistaken; perhaps he was insensitive and self-obsessed, after all.

She took one last look around the village. A donkey, ear awry, stood patiently by a wall; the silent men clicked their beads and watched. At the end of the street was a small black car with two men inside, looking as if they were dozing in the heat.

Dean sped away from the village with a spurt of gravel when Sally had barely settled on her seat.

'Hey, what's the hurry?' she called out.

'Just hang on—and don't look back.'

Curiosity overcame her fear, and Sally glanced behind them, down the steep and bumpy road. The small black car was following them. She frowned in surprise to see it.

Dean turned off the paved road on to a dirt track which demanded all his driving skills. Dust rose from the rapidly spinning wheels as they climbed. On one side was a precipitous drop several hundred feet to a ravine below; on the other a steep slope dotted with pine trees. The stone-strewn track they were following became a footpath, and they bumped their way ever upwards between the trees. There was no way a car could follow them here, even a small one.

'Is this really necessary?' she had called out at one particularly hair-raising moment, but Dean did not reply.

Sally clung to him, trying to use her weight to help balance the bike, and prayed desperately for the nightmare to be over.

When the bike eventually did stop, she heard Dean say, 'It's OK now, you can open your eyes.' She straightened her legs and climbed off the bike, stretching painfully.

'Well, what do you think? I said I'd take you somewhere special for lunch.' They were not quite at the top of the mountain, standing in a wide, grassy meadow. The view was breathtaking, across forest and valley to more mountains.

Nearby was a small white building with a high, blue dome, a bell tower with a rope and bell intact.

'It's spectacular,' she said. 'Utterly beautiful—but, Dean, what was all that about back there?'

CHAPTER FIVE

'Let's get something to eat first—I talk better over a glass of wine,' Dean suggested.

'OK, but at the chapel?'

'Better than that.' Dean opened the panniers on the bike and took out an ice box, then led the way to a shady spot at the edge of the meadow. In the box were a bottle of wine, some bread and cheese, and tomatoes and fruit. 'Not very imaginative,' he said. 'But the wine should be good.'

'I hope you've remembered the corkscrew—and it looks great. I'm starving.' Sally began to help lay out the picnic.

'Fortunately, I've got a Swiss Army knife.'

'I wouldn't expect anything less from you,' Sally teased, as he began to search through the various blades of the wonder knife. 'But are we safe now, eating here? There won't be stray bullets passing overhead at any moment?'

'I'm pretty certain of it. They were only following us, not trying to kill us.'

'I'm glad to hear it. I wish you'd told me about it before.'

'Come on, help yourself to some food. Anyway, where's your British stiff upper lip?'

'I left it down the dirt track somewhere!'

'Yes, I'm sorry I had to cut in on what you were telling me about your friend Paul. Tell me the rest now. I do want to know—it's just that then I thought we ought to get moving.'

'Uh-huh.' Sally shook a finger at him. 'No sidetracking. Your story comes first, this time.'

Dean drank some wine, then gazed speculatively at his glass for a moment. 'I don't know if you're going to believe me,' he began, and Sally groaned.

'Don't tell me they're pressmen determined to photograph your latest female conquest.'

Dean laughed. 'Why on earth would journalists be interested in me? You've mentioned that before, but I thought it was a joke.'

'Well, the story is that you're some kind of playboy millionaire trying to live the reclusive life here.'

Dean stopped laughing and sat up straight, with crossed legs and a serious expression on his face. 'I'm sorry Sally, the rumour is wrong—I can't think how it got started. If you think that, by tagging along with me, diamonds and pearls are going to fall into your lap, you'd better leave now because they're not.'

'I thought no such thing,' she countered indignantly. 'In fact, I'm glad to learn you're an ordinary guy, like the rest of us.'

'Fine—only less of the ordinary, please. I like to think myself—'

'Extraordinary, I know,' Sally finished for

65

him. 'I suppose I forgive you for branding me a gold digger, even if for only five seconds, but answer me this—how come you've got a yacht all of your own, *and* a parcel of Greek land?'

'I worked hard and saved money. It was always my dream to own a yacht, so that I could be free to come and go whenever I wanted to. Of course, nothing these days is completely free—you still have to fill in forms when you go in and out of harbours, and register with the local police. I hate all this twentieth-century bureaucracy.'

'So you're a cowboy at heart!' Sally said delightedly.

'Not quite—I'm a city boy born and bred. But it's my hatred of all that paperwork, plus some kind of smuggling going on locally that's made difficulty between the police and me on one or two occasions. We've had one or two arguments.' He held up a bunched fist. 'You could say I've made myself kinda unpopular around here.'

* * *

Sally rolled over on to her stomach, and studied the patch of grass by her elbow. She was disquieted by what Dean had told her. The facts fitted whichever way you looked at them—right down to the surliness of Simon, his only crew. Was he standing by a wrongly accused friend and respected adult, or was he,

66

too, trying to cover up? Innocent or guilty? She supposed it came down to a matter of trust, in which case was it him she should trust or her own instincts—which had not always helped her in the past?

She looked up, more questions on her lips, and found Dean reclining on his side, and his face only inches from hers. He put out a hand and touched her cheek, studying her face for a second before pulling her towards him.

She was aware that somewhere a grasshopper ticked in the grass, and that above them the leaves of a shady tree were rustling in a breeze, sending little patches of sunlight dappling across them. Then she was no longer even aware of anything except Dean's lips on hers, sending tremors of delight coursing through her body. She closed her eyes, giving herself up to his kiss, all the doubts and questions of a moment before quite forgotten. His mouth was warm and insistent on hers, his hand tracing a path down her neck, caressing her . . . Then, seconds later, he withdrew it and sat up.

Sally opened her eyes again, and instantly saw what had caused Dean to draw away—a flock of sheep was passing by, accompanied by a whistling shepherd and his dog. Unhurriedly they both sat up and watched the sheep pass by on a lower slope, followed by the old man; his face tanned to the colour and consistency of leather. He wore a black muslin handkerchief twisted round his wisp of white hair, and his clothes were an odd ragbag mixture of garments. When he saw them, he lifted his stick and called out to them. They waved back.

'You don't think that's one of your policemen in disguise?' asked Sally.

'Do you mean the shepherd or a sheep?'

Laughing, they collected their belongings and began to pack them away.

Sally was glad, in a way, for the interruption. At the moment her relationship with Dean Samuelson hung in the balance, and she was reluctant for anything to be added in his favour until she felt absolutely sure her trust was not misplaced.

As they made ready to mount the Suzuki, Sally laid a hand on Dean's arm.

'Have the police any real reason to be suspicious of you?' she asked. 'You're not a smuggler, are you?'

For answer he looked deep into her eyes, then leaned forward and planted a gentle kiss upon her mouth. 'I promise you, I've done nothing that the police could take exception to.'

'But where is it you go to, when you're not running trips for SunSea? I looked for the *Dolphin* in Theopolis harbour the other day, but she wasn't there.' Sally immediately regretted her words as a set expression appeared on Dean's face. Somehow she had angered him, although he was suppressing it.

Of course—all that talk about freedom, and here she was trying to put tabs on him.

'I just went out sailing, that's all. I enjoy it, remember? Now, will you be OK for the return journey? We're taking the proper road down, so it won't be so bumpy.'

Sally held Dean tightly again as they bumped their way towards the road. Neither of them noticed the bright flash in a clump of trees far to their left as if the sun had caught on a piece of glass, or perhaps the lenses of a pair of binoculars.

*   *   *

This time Sally found riding on the motor bike exhilarating. She was able to remember the good times she had shared with Paul, although she wished that he, too, was still able to smell the scent of thyme in the warm air and enjoy the blue brilliance of the day.

However, her thoughts were busy, too, on everything Dean had told her. Perhaps she had been right the very first time they had met, and he was a shy artist. She knew for sure, however, that if she tried to probe further, Dean would close up like a clam. As long as she took him at face value—good for a kiss by moonlight, a few laughs—he was hers. But for how long? And why did she sense that this was only a front he was putting on—for her benefit or for someone else's? The trouble was, she

69

knew she was on the verge of wanting more, and yet if she were to push forward would Dean then feel he was being put in a cage? Hadn't he made it plain that he was footloose and fancy free, and wanted to remain that way?

Dean stopped in the main square of Xora village, and Sally climbed off the back of the bike, her legs stiff again.

Dean remained seated.

'Thanks for a wonderful day,' she said, 'even though it was more exciting than I bargained for.'

'I enjoyed it too,' he said, then paused. Sally felt that he was going to prolong their time together and her heart quickened in anticipation. But he went on to say, 'Will you be taking the next trip over to Micro Aspro? That's on Thursday, this week.'

'I'm not sure—see if I can arrange it.'

'Good.' They smiled at one another, Sally hiding her disappointment, then Dean kissed her on the forehead. 'Meanwhile, you have a keepsake to remember me by, don't you?'

'What's that?' Sally asked, her mind a blank.

'So much for mementoes! That strange coin or medallion I found on Micro Aspro.'

'Oh, yes.'

'I thought you'd be wearing it round your neck,' he teased her lightly, tracing with his forefinger the skin just around the neck of her T-shirt. 'Where has the age of romance gone?'

'I'd intended to have a hole put in it but it disappeared, Dean. I don't know how or where. I searched my bedroom very carefully, but I think someone must have stolen it.'

'Stolen it?' Dean removed his hand and took her firmly by the shoulders. 'Are you sure?'

'Yes, quite sure. I'm so sorry.'

'Forget the coin, that's of no consequence. It's you I'm thinking of. Did you report the break-in?'

Sally shook her head. 'No, there didn't seem much point. It was the night of the disco, you remember, and I'd left it on my dressing-table. When I got back it was gone, and I found that my clothes were disturbed as if someone had looked through my drawers.'

'I don't like the idea of people breaking into your room. I think you should tell the police.'

'But what could they do? One old piece of metal gone, and a few rumpled clothes. All the important things were still there. Now I keep my documents and camera in the office safe, and put a chair against my door at night.'

Dean grinned mischievously. 'I'll remember that if I decide to pay you a visit at midnight. But I want you to promise to take care of yourself. I want you on the *Dolphin* on Thursday, not found washed up on some beach.'

'I can look after myself,' Sally said briskly.

'Yeah, so you say—I bet you couldn't hurt

a fly!' He looked at her closely. 'And nothing else odd has happened?'

Sally frowned. 'No, not that I can think of. What do you mean by "odd"?'

'I don't know—only sometimes men can get a fixation on a girl, follow her around. Sometimes that can be dangerous.'

'I can promise you, no one's been following me. You're the one who has to keep looking over his shoulder.'

'You're right. And my own fault, too, for not sticking strictly to the rules. Well, I have to get going now, back to Theopolis.'

*   *   *

Sally rested one hand lightly on his arm. 'Dean, one more thing. You know that coin—I saw some more of them in the museum. They're very old, and it was probably valuable. There might be more of them on Micro Aspro. You could probably claim treasure trove or something.'

'Is that so.' Dean gave a low whistle. 'Maybe I'll try to find some more. But what were you doing in a museum? I thought you never went near the places.'

'All in the line of duty, a SunSea trip. Anyway, I'm trying to change my ways—you've broadened my mind.'

'I must do it more often.' He kissed her on the cheek, then kicked the bike into life and

72

roared away.

Sally began to stroll back towards her room. What a weird day it had been. Yet, with Dean's help, she had managed to overcome her dread of motor bikes, and had been able to talk about Paul without too much pain. She hadn't finished her tale, but that didn't matter. Yes, she was beginning to face up to things, and perhaps one day she would be able to accept that she had made a mistake, she had failed Paul, but that it wouldn't happen again.

Dean had shown that he cared for her today, but then, she could imagine him supporting any number of people—as long as there were no strings attached. 'I love to be free to roam wherever I want,' he'd said. Sally determined not to let this new insight into his character cast her down. For the time being he enjoyed being with her, and she knew that Dean was very special to her. Somehow they might be able to continue the balancing act they had begun.

Sally was loath to stay shut up in her room on such a beautiful evening so she took her cheque book and purse with her and set off to look for presents for her family and friends. Despite the fact that it was Sunday— the church bell was sounding out its single, rhythmic note—most of the shops would be open till late.

She knew quite a few people now, and enjoyed exchanging a word here and there with the villagers of Xora as she passed by them, as well as SunSea holidaymakers out for their own evening stroll. It seemed to her that the colours were brighter than usual, the scents sharper in her nostrils, and she glowed with a sense of well-being.

She browsed through shelf after shelf of ceramics, leatherware, delicate, shimmering shells. She bought a pair of plates for her mother, a leather bag for Sue, as requested, and could not resist buying a large whorled conch shell for herself.

Outside in the street, she blinked in the sudden brightness after the dim interior of the shop she had just left. Then she spotted a stall up a narrow alleyway. She hadn't been there before, and climbed the shallow stone steps up to it. In an open tray she found some coins, old pieces of coral and modern jewellery, all mixed in together.

An overweight Greek man with dark curly hair came and stood in the doorway. He wore the light blue short-sleeved shirt and casual grey trousers that was the usual Greek summer dress, and he was smoking a cigarette. He barely glanced at Sally, apparently unconcerned whether she should spend money or not.

Her appetite whetted she asked, 'Is there more inside?'

He stood to one side, gesturing her in, but did not follow her. He seemed more interested in what was happening down the street. Sally discovered, to her amazement, that the inside of the shop was an Aladdin's cave. Firmly locked away under glass were expensive items of gold and silver, and on the counter a sign indicating that most international credit cards were accepted.

*   *   *

After hesitating over a small silver ring set with a topaz, which she couldn't really afford, her gaze fell on another display case, partly hidden by a revolving stand of leather belts. She stooped to examine it—and her spine tingled in recognition.

Here were the most expensive items in the shop—antique jewellery from all over the world—and there was her coin! She was sure of it; it had a chip in its edge in the same place. But when she looked again, and saw several others, all very similar, she had to admit that it probably wasn't the one that had been stolen from her room.

All the same, when she read the price tag she almost gasped. It couldn't be worth that much, surely? But if so, no wonder the burglar hadn't looked for anything else—just one of those was well worth his foray into her room.

She sensed a movement behind her and, thinking it was the shop owner, perhaps wary of the length of time she'd been looking at his most costly goods, stepped away from the case. But instead of the fat Greek, who still lounged in the doorway with a fresh cigarette, she found herself looking into the dark features of Peter Elsing.

'Hello, Sally,' he said, sounding really pleased to see her. 'Sorry if I startled you.'

'No, you didn't. I was making good my escape before I was tempted to buy.'

'Fantastic shop, isn't it? I only discovered it the other day, and you're the only other person I've seen in here. But he must do a good trade.'

'This is the first time I've been here, too. It's funny how you can find new places, even in a village as small as Xora.'

'That's one of its delights, of course. What also happens is that you lose track of people entirely. I haven't seen you for days.'

'Being a holiday rep involves quite a lot of work, I've found.'

'And I thought you were on holiday. Well, the item I was looking for has been sold. Why don't we have a drink, if you're free.'

Sally had lost her initial wariness of the Englishman. He seemed harmless enough, and she had bought a fair number of presents already, so she agreed.

They nodded to the shop owner as they left, but he ignored them, flicking his cigarette stub across the street.

'Are you staying in Xora?' asked Sally as

they ordered their drinks.

'No. The film company are extremely generous with my expenses, and they've put me in the Xora Heights Hotel, just outside the village.'

'What's it like? I've only seen it when driving past.'

'Luxurious! Marble floors, a swimming pool, a restaurant, but only a handful of people staying there. I almost wish I was in the village.'

'Yes, it's more fun in the village,' Sally agreed.

'And have you had time to explore the island yet?'

'I have.' Sally sketched in what she had seen that day, but did not mention Dean, nor that they had been followed. 'I know the church you mean—it was a thriving monastery once. But what about the really old sites?'

'None,' confessed Sally. 'Although I've been to the museum.'

'Interesting, but not like seeing the real places. While I've been looking at locations for the film, I've been able to follow up my own enthusiasms.'

'How did you get the job?'

'They advertised in an archaeological magazine, of all things, and we lecturers often take summer jobs, if we're not working on a book or article.'

'And what have you found so far?'

'Two superb places. One is a grove which was used for sacred worship to the gods. The other is a ruined village, built on a rocky headland, empty now apart from lizards. I've made notes, taken photos, and sent reports back to England.'

'They worshipped Poseidon, didn't they?'

'That's right. The sea plays strange tricks around here, although it looks calm enough, and so they needed to placate it.'

'Did they make sacrifices? Of fish, perhaps?'

Peter laughed, showing small, even white teeth. 'No, the occasional lamb or chicken, that's all. Nothing sinister.'

Then he drew closer and lowered his voice. 'In fact, I've found a few items and taken them to my room to make notes for an article I want to write. I knew that Kouros had some interesting items—it was me who suggested to the film company to come here.'

Sally could easily believe that Peter's persuasive manner had worked in his favour over their choice of island. 'So you're killing two birds with one stone,' she said.

'Exactly.'

'But aren't you supposed to hand everything in that you find?'

'Yes, and I will—after I've had a good look first. Why don't you come and see them? I'll buy you lunch at the hotel.'

Sally was more curious about the hotel than she was about Peter's 'finds', and she also realised that he desperately wanted someone to talk to.

'Thanks. Will tomorrow be all right?'

As they talked the light had gradually faded. Sally had arranged to meet Fiona and Donna for supper if she was back, so she said goodbye to Peter.

As she walked through the village she knew she was glad she had bumped into Peter. Now she was alone again she found she was missing Dean already. It seemed a long time to wait until Thursday, when she would see him again.

CHAPTER SIX

Sally found she had plenty of work to do the next day. Donna had to go into Theopolis to visit the main bank, and Fiona had sent a message to say that she was unwell. The message arrived before Donna left, and she frowned.

'That's the third time this week,' she said. 'I hope it's nothing serious.'

'She was very quiet yesterday evening, I thought.'

'You noticed too? I wondered if she had something on her mind.'

'Possibly, but I didn't think she was unhappy, did you? And I think she told me some time ago she suffered from migraines.'

'That's true.' Donna looked unconvinced. 'All the same, I think I had better look into it when I get back. Normally Fiona is so conscientious and cheerful, I wouldn't like to think that there was something wrong, and she was worrying about it.'

Donna picked up her bag and folder, ready to leave. 'Will you be all right on your own?'

'I'm sure I will,' Sally reassured her. 'I feel I've learned a lot in the last month, and we don't seem to have any Grundeys at the moment.'

Donna smiled. 'Thank goodness! Well, I'd better go, or I'll miss the nine o'clock bus.'

Sally remembered Peter's invitation to lunch as Donna was going out of the door, and ran after her. 'Will it be all right for me to close the office for a couple of hours at lunchtime? I've been invited to the Xora Heights Hotel.'

'I don't see why not. Leave a note on the door about your whereabouts in case of emergencies. You must tell me what the place is like. It only opened this year, and I haven't visited it yet. Who are you meeting?'

'A man called Peter Elsing, a lecturer. Do you remember him—at the disco?'

'That man with the dark hair?'

Donna suddenly grinned and tapped Sally on the arm. 'Don't let Dean Samuelson know about your tryst!'

'What's he got to—' Sally began to protest,

80

but Donna was already hurrying away.

Sally shook her head and smiled. She knew Donna had been joking and, anyway, she had no objection to her name being linked with Dean's. But why had Peter Elsing invited her? Was it really only that he was lonely? Or that he wanted to show her the things he had found?

She was not given any time to ponder the question further. There was a steady stream of holidaymakers with queries that morning. Where could they buy English newspapers, was the tap water drinkable, where was the best place to hire a car? Sally felt more than satisfied with her morning's work by the time she locked up the office.

*   *   *

It was a very hot day. She had become accustomed to the cloudless days and warm nights being made bearable by the sea breeze, but today seemed even hotter than usual. There was a slight haze, which made the sun appear bigger and more fiery. As she walked through the village, having pinned up a note about her whereabouts, people were already beginning to gather in shady tavernas for their lunch, out of the glare of the sun.

The mid-day sun had shrunk the shadows of trees along the road, and the tar at its edges was melting. Insects buzzed in the dry, yellow

81

grass, and even the tiny lizards were keeping well hidden in the dark crevices of the rocks. Sally walked slowly up the hill away from the village, her thoughts fixed on a long cold drink filled with large chunks of ice.

The Xora Heights Hotel was a striking, three-storey building with balconies running the width of its façade so that each room had one. There was a path leading down to a small rocky bay, private to the hotel, and in front was a wide, paved area. Sally crossed it swiftly on her way to the stone steps which led into the cool interior.

Peter was waiting for her, lounging against the reception desk, chatting to the pretty, dark-haired receptionist. He wore a white shirt, open at the neck with its sleeves rolled up to reveal dark-haired, wiry arms. He waved, said something to the receptionist in Greek, then came forward and pressed her hand energetically.

'Too hot today, eh? Come and sit by the pool and we'll order something cold to drink.'

He led the way across the reception area, up some steps and through smoked glass doors to the back of the hotel. There were tables and umbrellas set all around the pool, but only one other couple sat out there. Grey-haired and bronzed, their table bearing empty glasses, books, camera and papers, they did not even look up as Sally and Peter sat down under an umbrella by the pool's edge.

Sally thankfully slid off her sandals and put her feet into the cool water.

'Wonderful,' she said. Then, after looking around, went on, 'I see what you mean—there's hardly anybody here.'

'There are others, but they're mostly out for the day. Luxurious though, isn't it?'

The waiter arrived with their drinks, and Sally drank half a glass of orange juice at a gulp.

'Next week, though, the place will come alive. The film crew arrives—the whole shebang,' Peter announced. Sally realised he was proud of his connection with the film.

'Really? They're going to stay here, near Xora? What about the actors? Is anybody famous in the film?'

''Fraid not. Mostly unknowns, chosen for their muscles and looks. I expect there'll be a party. Why don't you and your friends come, too?'

'Thanks, we'd love to,' Sally accepted, although as she did so she wondered whether Peter was pretending greater influence than he actually had. For his sake, she did not press for further details.

'In fact, as I suggested, they're arriving earlier than originally intended.'

'Oh? Why's that?'

'This festival in the mountains—I expect you know all about it. Are you organising a coach party to it?'

'I've not heard anything about it. But do go on, it sounds as if we should.'

'Yes, it's quite a big gathering—lots of eating and drinking, folk dancing, the wearing of old costumes. Apparently the most influential families on the island always go, so I thought it might be useful for the film folk to make contact, especially if they are going to need extras or access to private land.'

'That sounds a good idea—and thanks for telling me about it. It may be that Donna has something organised but, if not, it should be ideal for an evening out.'

*   *   *

Peter and Sally dined in splendid solitude in the vast, highly polished dining-room with its black and white chequered floor, and a nosegay of flowers decorating their table. They ate a tasty meal of stuffed peppers, grilled fish and salad, washed down with plenty of chilled white wine.

As the waiter took their empty plates away, Peter said, 'Let's have coffee sent up to my room—I'm looking forward to your reaction to my "finds". I'm sure you'll be interested.'

Peter's enthusiasm was infectious, and Sally understood how much he must have wanted to share his discoveries with someone. His room was on the first floor, and was large and tastefully furnished. The windows to the balcony stood open, and it was cool there.

However, once they were inside, Peter turned and locked the door.

Seeing her look of surprised dismay, he smiled and handed her the key. 'A minor precaution only,' he explained. 'We'll have plenty of warning when the man brings the coffee, so we'll have time to hide the things.'

Sally pocketed the key, but kept her fist closed round it loosely. Peter was making a great deal of fuss about the artefacts he'd picked up. Of course, having seen some of the prices on them, she could understand why he was taking care that no one knew he had them so that they wouldn't be stolen. Or was he simply trying to make himself appear more important in her eyes?

Peter had hidden the pieces in a suitcase, under some clothes, and when he took them out he handled them lovingly, almost reverently. It was difficult for her to tell what they were—the first items he showed her looked just like knobbly pieces of stone with no real shape. But Peter explained how this was half of a jar, that was a die for casting coins, and that was used for cooking— and Sally began to get an inkling of their fascination, began to see how they were parts of a jigsaw, a puzzle to be solved.

'But the most interesting thing I discovered only last night,' Peter was saying excitedly, his eyes burning with an almost fanatical gleam.

'It was listed in this book, too.' He held up a thick, new volume, its pages densely packed with type and extensive footnotes. 'The people of Kouros worshipped a more primitive version of Poseidon before visitors from the mainland brought a more sophisticated god with them. We're talking about several thousand years BC, now. Here's the sketch I made of the sacred grove.'

He held it out for Sally to see, while continuing to finger something in the suitcase.

'Really, how interesting,' she murmured, trying but failing to share his enthusiasm. The drawing reminded her of the one that had fallen out of Dean's bag that day they had met.

'But wait until you see what I'm going to show you now, then you'll understand. Such a find! And I'll get my article first into print about it—it could open up whole areas of new research. It will make my name.'

'Oh?' Sally put down the unremarkable drawing and waited, but hardly with bated breath, for what Peter was about to show her. 'Really,' she thought to herself, 'all the fuss he's making about something that happened five thousand years ago. What does it matter?' But it wasn't worth arguing with him, he was completely hooked.

Peter now lifted a scarred and corroded piece of metal out of the case, handling it as if it was made of eggshell, and Sally saw that it had some shapes cut out of it.

'It was a ritual mask worn by the priests of the early inhabitants of Kouros,' he explained. 'Like this.' And he held it up in front of his face, so that she could see the eye and mouth holes. It looked hideous.

'Ugh,' Sally shuddered. 'I bet the priests were able to frighten people with one of those on. Perhaps they frightened the sea god with it!'

'Not quite, but close.' Peter still held the mask in front of his face. 'When they wore it they *became* the god. Do you see?'

'I suppose so—ah, here's the coffee.' Sally was very relieved to hear loud knocking at the door. She thought Peter was behaving distinctly oddly; the mask seemed to bring out the worst in him. She hurried over to the door, calling out in Greek while Peter muttered, 'Wait, I must hide them away.'

When the waiter came in he looked from one to the other of them, obviously disapproving, although he could see nothing amiss. Sally hoped he wouldn't gossip about them being together in the bedroom like this with the door locked. She wished she hadn't agreed so impulsively to Peter's plans.

'Let's go out on to the balcony,' she suggested. 'And then I must go. I've lots of work to do this afternoon.'

'Shame SunSea must be slave drivers.' Peter seemed to have returned to normal now he had hidden the case away again, but he continued to talk for a short while about his article, although it meant little to Sally.

As she descended the hill back to the village, Sally knew that she would try to avoid being alone with Peter Elsing again. She also hoped that he had told her the truth, and that the film people would be arriving soon. He shouldn't be alone for long.

*   *   *

At the end of the afternoon, Sally thankfully closed the SunSea office and wandered aimlessly down to the beach. She took off her sandals and paddled along the edge of the sea, enjoying the feel of firm wet sand beneath her feet. She found she was walking in the direction of the beach where Dean had found her, and as she did so an idea formed in her mind.

Why not follow the track that led behind the seashore, towards the land that Dean had bought? She was very curious to see it, and perhaps he might be there . . .

The heat of the day had worn off, but she was warm enough in her white cotton sundress. A light breeze stirred her hair as she walked along the road. It was paved but had plenty of potholes. Olive trees lined the roadside, and the reddish ground beyond them was strewn with grey-white rocks amid golden brown stalks of desiccated grass. Sally, walking in alternate light and shade, heard a rustle and thought of snakes, but instead a tethered goat raised its head and bleated at her.

The road was deserted and after a while she began to wonder if her spur of the moment idea was such a good one. What could she do if she came across unwanted company here? Hadn't Dean warned her that someone— the burglar—might be interested in her? She glanced around fearfully, but saw no one.

Then again, supposing she succeeded in finding Dean's land, and he was there, would he be pleased to see her? She tried to imagine a happy expression on his face, but all she could conjure up was a frowning grimace as he said, 'I told you to keep away.'

She stopped. She had been walking for about twenty minutes and must be halfway there by now; there were glimpses of the sea through the trees to her left. Should she go on or turn back?

The fact that she was nearly there drove her on. And honesty compelled her to admit that she very much wanted to see Dean again—and had more than a passing interest in the land he owned.

Shortly afterwards there was a break in the trees on the seaward side of the road, and a rough track leading off. Down below she could see a chain fence, and went to investigate. There was a gate, without a padlock, and a sign in Greek which she could not understand. She went in, following the path where tyremarks indicated recent activity.

She had not gone far, her skin crawling with the uneasy sensation that she was being watched, when someone called out: 'Sally—what are you doing here?' She looked round and saw Dean standing on some rocks to her right.

'Hi,' she called. 'I thought I'd pay you a surprise visit as I had nothing better to do.'

He loped effortlessly down from the rocks and came to stand beside her. He was wearing a white T-shirt and very old Levis, both stained with dirt.

'If I'd known you were coming, I'd have changed—or at least had a wash.' He grinned, seeing her look of amazement. 'But, Sally, you shouldn't have come here. Do I have to repeat myself about reading signs?'

'I couldn't make head or tail of the one on the gate. I just guessed this was the right place. What does the sign say?'

'Entry strictly forbidden, or words to that effect.'

'But what's the attraction of this place? It looks pretty wild to me,' Sally asked, looking around at the desolate landscape.

'Oh, it's much prettier down by the sea.'

'Is that where you're working? Can I see?' Sally asked with interest.

Dean shook his head. 'You guessed right—I was working. But I'd rather you didn't see yet.

I want it to be a surprise.'

'Is it a house—a villa?'

'What? Oh yes, a villa, that's definitely what it is. And now I'm going to walk you back to Xora. You must be crazy coming all this way on your own. It's asking for trouble.'

'Yes, I had a feeling I was being watched around here.'

'That was probably Simon. He saw you coming and told me. How else do you think I found you?'

*   *   *

They had reached the highway again, and Dean put his arm casually round her shoulders in a friendly fashion.

'I'm sorry if I've disturbed you—and I still can't see the attraction in that scrubland.'

'I'm glad you came. Thursday was beginning to seem a long way off. Now, tell me what you've been doing.'

'I bought some presents and souvenirs yesterday, and today I had lunch at the Xora Heights Hotel.' Once the words were out, she regretted them. She recalled Dean's antipathy to her lunch companion too late, and finished lamely, 'With Peter Elsing.'

His arm tightened. 'Not him again. What do you see in him?'

'I had thought he was just lonely, but now I think he's obsessed with ancient history. You should see the way his eyes light up when he talks about having a scoop on something that happened three thousand years ago.'

Dean laughed. 'Did you give him a hard time like you did me?'

'No. I felt that he wouldn't even hear me.'

'You know what I think of him—I'd suggest you keep away.'

'I probably will—although he's invited me and Donna and Fiona to the film company's party when they arrive this week.'

Dean was silent for a moment and then when he spoke his tone was light. 'Well, it's up to you. You're a free woman.'

Dean left her near Xora, after kissing her on the cheek, and returned the way they'd come. Although he'd seemed genuinely pleased to see her, she felt decidedly deflated. Perversely she was disappointed at being told she had her freedom. Didn't he care if she saw other men?

Allied to that was an odd sensation that, although she trusted him, she still didn't believe he was telling the full story about himself.

*　　　*　　　*

During the night the heat increased until it became an oppressive, stifling blanket. A haze obscured the sky, and the air teemed with insects and flying ants. Fiona had returned to work assuring Sally and Donna that she was completely recovered, but the heat made them all three feel listless.

After a particularly abusive exchange with a recalcitrant plumber, Donna slammed the phone down, and said, 'Let's shut up shop and go and sit in Nicos' taverna with a cold drink. I can't take any more.' She ran her fingers through her hair as she spoke, lifting it away from her perspiring forehead.

Fiona and Sally were only too glad to sit at their favourite table, sipping a drink lazily through straws, watching the harbour.

'Have you noticed, all the boats are in?' Fiona remarked.

'Did you see those small white clouds this morning?' Donna asked by way of reply. 'I think we may be in for a storm. There were some this time last year—it's peculiar to Kouros.'

A long, low rumble in the distance sounded right on cue. 'There it is—thunder.'

A wind had sprung up while they were sitting there, and now it grew stronger, bringing with it black clouds that filled the sky, leaving only a strip of brightness on the horizon. Then lightning split the darkness, followed by a crack of thunder that resounded above the village.

'Are we safe here?' asked Fiona a little fearfully.

Nicos appeared and beckoned them inside, bolting the door and securing the shutters.

Just in time, for the first large drops of rain were spattering the dust. Within minutes, a torrential downpour was drenching everything.

Escapees from the beach ran for their rooms and villas, a few still in beachwear. Gutters overflowed, the streets became rushing streams, flowers and plants were broken and bent while above the lightning flashed and thunder reverberated.

'Fantastic. I love storms,' said Donna.

'Well, I hate them,' wailed Fiona. 'This is worse than last year.'

'It'll clear the air, anyway,' Sally pointed out.

'I hope your Colin is flying above this,' Fiona said to Donna. 'And I wish it would hurry up and go away.'

'He'll be back in England at the moment, having bacon and eggs and looking at the drizzle, I expect. But I pity any poor sailor out there. Dean's in port, isn't he, Sally?'

Sally felt her heart quicken. 'He didn't say he was going out in the *Dolphin* today, but he's a law unto himself.'

'Oh, I expect he's listened to the weather forecast. He's a very experienced sailor.'

All the same, Sally was relieved when, quite soon, the wind blew the clouds out to sea. Apart from an occasional glimpse of lightning, the storm was over. The air was clear and fresh. Kouros was cleansed.

CHAPTER SEVEN

The storm was followed by another, equally violent, the next day. Sally, who had been asked to collect the new arrivals that day, saw the bemused looks on the faces of the incoming holidaymakers as, dressed in light clothing, they had to dash from the airport building into a waiting coach. She hastened to reassure them that the bad weather would soon be gone, and they need not regret leaving their umbrellas in England. Sure enough, by the time they arrived in Xora, the village was bathed in sunshine.

There had been storm damage, however, Sally noticed during the journey. Boulders had tumbled down on to the main road, the usually dried-up riverbeds had swollen, and the crops in the fields looked badly bruised and battered. As far as Sally knew, no one had actually been hurt, and the only destruction in Xora was one fishing boat which had torn free from its moorings and lay smashed on the rocks down the coast.

The newcomers seemed to be a jolly crowd except for one man who was dressed in a lightweight suit and tie which marked him apart from the others, and also wore black-rimmed glasses. He sat silently on his own during the coach ride, as if deliberately withdrawing from the people around him. His name was Arthur Sims, and when Sally showed him to his accommodation, she addressed him politely as Mr. Sims. He had taken a studio for two entirely for himself, and merely grunted when she explained where everything was. He came momentarily alive when she gave him the brochure listing the trips on offer.

'This one,' he said, jabbing the paper with his forefinger. 'When's that?'

'It should be tomorrow,' she replied when she saw that he was pointing at the trip to Micro Aspro.

'Should be? You're not sure?' He glared at her from behind his glasses, which magnified his eyes.

'It will depend on the weather. It would be too dangerous to go out if a storm was forecast.'

'Mmm,' he accepted this point. 'Put me down for it, or whatever it is you do.' And then he turned away without thanking her or saying goodbye, and began to unpack his one small suitcase.

As she walked back to the office, Sally wondered what Arthur Sims was doing on Kouros. He was completely unlike the other holidaymakers. He was uninterested in his surroundings, yet was keen to go on a trip. Mention of the beach and watersports facilities had only elicited an irritated shake of the head. Perhaps he would surprise her by

96

turning up in bermuda shorts and announcing he was an amateur naturalist.

Donna, wearing a white broderie anglaise cotton dress that showed off her dark red hair and red-brown tan, was looking harassed when Sally reported to her at the office.

'How did it go?' she asked.

'No problems, although the storm brought a few funny remarks.'

'Oh, the weather will settle down again soon enough. Although I admit Kouros' weather is different to other islands.'

She was looking down at some papers in her hand, shuffling through them without really seeing them, Sally could tell.

'Is everything all right?' she asked. 'Where's Fiona?'

'I can't understand her. She's never been like this before. She told me she was feeling sick at lunchtime, and asked for the afternoon off. I don't think we'll see her at the party this evening, either, so we'll have to manage on our own.'

Sally sat down in the chair by her desk. 'Did you have that talk with her?'

Donna shook her head. 'I managed to snatch a few hours with Colin yesterday afternoon, and it went right out of my mind. Then when I saw her today—well, I don't want to call her a liar. She's a friend now.'

'Would you like me to look in on her to see if she's OK?'

'That would be wonderful. I've got so much to do this evening.'

'By the way, will tomorrow's trip be on? And is it OK if I take it? One of the new arrivals was asking about it already.'

'I spoke to Dean Samuelson on the phone earlier, and he said the forecast is for calm weather so he'll be here. Why, what's the matter?'

*   *   *

Sally's expression had given her away.

In the aftermath of the storm she had worried about Dean's safety, and had asked the coach driver to take her the long way round to the airport, past Theopolis harbour, where she'd fruitlessly searched for sight of the *Dolphin*.

'I'm glad to hear he's safe, that's all.'

'If you ask me, Dean's got nine lives. You don't need to worry about him.'

'What makes you say that?' Sally asked with interest.

'Well—there's not much to tell, really. But just before you arrived there was a big fight in Theopolis town, and Dean walked out of it with barely a scratch.'

'What was it about?'

'The police would like to know the answer to that one too! Some locals took it into their heads to attack Dean, or so he *says,* playing the innocent.'

Sally wanted to question Donna further, but to do so would mean revealing those things Dean had asked her to keep quiet about. She bit her lip, her loyalties divided, and remained silent.

The drinks party that night was a success, though Arthur Sims was notable by his absence. Afterwards, as Sally walked towards Sofia's house, she remembered her intention of checking whether Fiona was all right. Her room was on the ground floor of a villa inside its own walled garden. A lamp burned beside the courtyard door, but inside all was quiet and dark. The lemons on their tree were ghostly in the shadows.

The shutters on Fiona's windows were closed. Sally tapped on the door but there was no reply. She tried the handle, but the door was locked. She looked around, and noticed that the shutters were only pushed to, not bolted, and that there was a faint glimmer of light from one of the windows. She pulled it open and looked in, half-fearing to see Fiona lying collapsed on the floor, or lying deathly pale in bed.

A small table lamp was beside the bed, providing light enough to see the whole room. Shoes were lined up tidily beside the wardrobe, a dressing-gown lying neatly folded over a chair, and the bed was neatly made, too—and empty. Curious, Sally looked carefully around the room again. It looked as if it had not been used recently, yet the light was on. She wondered if she had made a mistake and this was not Fiona's room, but she recognised some of Fiona's things.

Sally knocked again, more loudly this time, in case Fiona was in the bathroom. But the door was open, and the light switched off. The whole villa remained silent. Perhaps Fiona had recovered and gone out for the evening after all.

But one thing puzzled Sally—the unnatural tidiness of her room. Last time she had seen it, it had been a mess, with clothes tangled on the floor and the bed unmade, while Fiona cheerfully explained that she didn't believe in wasting time over housework because everything got untidy again straight away. Could she have reformed in only a fortnight?

Pleased that Fiona had not been ill, Sally continued down an unfamiliar side street and then found herself climbing some steps under an archway. She was lost! She hesitated then, hearing voices and music, headed towards them.

She came to a small square, filled with lights and noise. An old pine grew in the centre, its feathery branches decorated with coloured light bulbs, and on all sides sat men and women, clapping and singing, while young Greek people, in costume, were dancing around the tree. Still in shadow, Sally paused to watch. An elderly loudspeaker, perched in the tree, relayed loud Greek music. As the dancers stepped and dipped to the intoxicating rhythm, Sally began to tap her foot. Then, as the circle came round again, she froze in surprise. For there was Fiona, dancing as light-footedly as any, laughing and radiant as if she hadn't a care in the world. Her dark curls bounced against the white of her costume.

Once more Sally's loyalties were torn. Had Fiona made a sudden recovery, and then joined this party—or had there been nothing wrong with her in the first place? But why keep it a secret? No one would have objected, or laughed at her, if she had wanted time off to learn Greek dancing.

She would have to ask her about it, but tomorrow not tonight. Sally was loath to break into the festivities, and so she quietly retraced her steps, away from the square.

Thursday dawned bright and clear. It was routine now for Sally to wait for the daytrippers to congregate on the jetty, while the motor boat stood ready to take them across to the yacht. The *Dolphin* was already in the bay when she arrived, blue and white prow high out of the water, sails billowing, as she pulled at anchor.

At last all fifteen were checked off on Sally's list, the last to arrive being Arthur Sims, wearing a small straw homburg-style hat to shade his eyes, a long-sleeved shirt and cardigan. He carried a white plastic bag. He muttered in reply to Sally's greeting, avoiding meeting her eyes. She led the way to the motorboat, and all fifteen squeezed in.

As the boat puttered smoothly through the water, Sally felt her stomach tighten in anticipation of seeing Dean. Despite his remark that he, too, thought Thursday a long way away, he had not made any effort to see her. When she had trekked off to see him that afternoon, she knew she had made it obvious to him that she was prepared to take their relationship a step further. While neither turning her away, nor making her feel foolish, he had left her with the feeling that all he sought was a romantic summer friendship.

If only she had been able to keep a tighter control on her feelings! Instead, she longed more than ever to see him, to be with him, despite the mystery she felt surrounded him. Or was it because of the mystery?

She was disappointed to find herself being helped on board by Simon. She caught the flicker of strong emotion in his eyes as he took her arm. Was it resentment or hatred?

'Hello, Simon,' she said. 'Thanks for spotting me the other day, otherwise I might have got lost.'

Simon stared at the ground as if he were stupid, and Sally laid a hand on his arm. 'What is it, Simon? Have I done something to upset you?'

He gave her another quick glare for answer, then sped away down the deck.

'No luck in getting through to him?' Dean spoke from behind her. 'Don't worry, you're not the only one.'

He was all in white—a white T-shirt that revealed his powerful muscles and showed off his even, brown tan, and white trousers. He was more attractive each time she saw him, she thought, and caught a faint scent of coconut sun oil mixed with his own personal scent.

'I wondered if I'd said something to annoy him,' she managed to say.

'Nothing at all,' he reassured her. 'He's suffering from the teenage blues, that's all. Sally, you look lovely today.'

'Thanks.' She looked up and met his eyes, and saw an answering spark there which made her heart flip over.

'We can't talk now,' he said in a quieter tone. 'Everyone's waiting for us to get going: Later, on the island.' He touched her arm briefly, the feel of his fingers on her skin sending a shiver down her spine.

The *Dolphin* glided through the water, the sea sparkled, and there was a stiff breeze. Arthur Sims stood alone, leaning over the rail, while Simon idly kicked his heels in the stern, deliberately ignoring Sally every time she passed near him. But she had eyes only for Dean, looking forward to the time they would be spending together, alone.

Dean held out his hand to help Sally down the steep bank of rocks to the shingle beach. The visit to the grotto was over, and everyone had spread out across the island for the afternoon so it had been easy for Dean and Sally to slip away together unnoticed for an hour.

When they sat down, Sally spoke first. 'Have you had any trouble with the police again, Dean?'

He gave a short laugh. 'You make me sound a real tearaway. No, I think they've given up on me at last. But we didn't come here to talk about my murky past. Here, lean on me.'

He put his arm around her and pulled her against his body, and she nestled comfortably against his chest.

'But Donna told me about the fight you were in a few weeks ago. You were lucky not to get hurt,' Sally persisted. 'Are you sure you've told me everything?'

'What do you mean by "everything"?' he said quietly, smoothing her hair.

'Dean—I care about you, about what happens to you. All the odd things that have happened, and that piece of land you're always scaring people away from—it doesn't add up.'

'So two and two make five occasionally?' he murmured against her cheek. 'Yet she says she cares for me. How British, but it'll do.' And he began to kiss her eyelids, the tip of her nose, her lips.

'Dean,' Sally protested weakly. 'Why won't you tell me—'

He stopped her mouth with his own, and she put her arms around his neck, twisting in his embrace as their lips melded together more urgently.

A rustling sound in the bushes behind them disturbed Sally, bringing her back to the present, and she broke free from his kiss. 'What's that? Did you hear something?'

'There's nothing there. Now, where was I?'

But Sally held a finger to his lips. 'You've managed to avoid answering my questions so far, but no longer,' she said.

'I know. But what makes you think—no, so darned certain—that there is anything to know?'

Sally frowned. 'It's more a feeling I have. I mean, I don't want to pry as I know how much you value your freedom. But don't you see, if you're in trouble, I'd like to help. I suppose that's all I want to say. You can count on me.'

Dean, instead of liking what she said, moved away from her and looked away. 'Sally, I have to ask you—why is it so important to you to find out? Assuming there is something to find out.'

'I thought I'd just told you—I care about you.'

He sighed. 'I wish I could believe that.'

'You sounded as if you did just now,' she said indignantly.

Now he was angry. 'I've told you before, I don't like being cross-examined. And if what you're saying is the truth, then how come you don't trust me?'

'But I do, that's the whole point. I wouldn't be here with you now if I didn't—there it is again. There's definitely something in the bushes.'

They both swung round, and Dean stood up. 'It's probably a bird,' he said. Then called out, 'Who's there?'

The leaves shook, branches were parted, then the straw hat and glasses of Arthur Sims appeared. He was pink and sweaty.

'What the hell—how long have you been there?' Dean took a threatening step towards him.

'I didn't know you were here,' said Arthur Sims belligerently. 'I only just got here.'

'We heard you moving about before. What's your game?'

'All right. All right, I'm going.' And he pushed clumsily away through the undergrowth.

'Leave it, Dean. I don't want trouble with yet another SunSea holidaymaker,' Sally said, getting up to stand beside him.

'Do you believe that?' he said angrily. 'He must have been watching us kissing.'

'Perhaps he thought he'd booked up for

"Peeping Tom Holidays". I thought he was a bit strange when he arrived,' Sally told him.

'He's weird, that guy.' Dean calmed down, then put his hands on her shoulders. 'Look, Sally, maybe I'm wrong, but until you trust me I don't think there's anything more to be said between us. Do you?'

Miserably, Sally met his eyes, but her appeal went unheeded.

*   *   *

The jetty was busy that afternoon. Sally had to inch her way past old fishermen with lined and leathery faces bent patiently over their net-mending, and over the coils of rope and fishing baskets which littered the wooden planks. But she hardly saw any of it. In her mind's eye she could only see the look on Dean's face.

After he had refused to meet her halfway, she had turned and hurried away, back to the beach where they had landed. He had not followed her. On the return journey she had sat with a noisy group, and Dean seemed intent only on the handling of the *Dolphin*, a stony expression on his face. Arthur Sims, on the other hand, had met her look full on, blankly, as if to say that it was she who was in the wrong, not him.

Donna was alone in the Sun Sea office when Sally arrived.

'Hello,' she said. 'How did the trip go?'

'So, so. Everybody seemed to enjoy themselves, much as usual.' 'Except me,' she thought.

'Good. Sit down a moment Sally, will you?'

'Uh-oh, that sounds like bad news. What's happened?'

'Nothing to worry about, but I feel I should tell you. I received notification from England that the Grundeys have lodged a complaint against you, and—'

'Oh, no. What did they say?'

'They claimed you were incompetent, and that you were endangering people's lives. I shall submit my own report now, and I expect the matter will drop there. After all, SunSea are grateful enough for the fact that you stepped into the breach, and couldn't expect you to be experienced within two weeks.'

'I'm not being withdrawn then?'

'No. It's possible that they'll investigate for themselves, but I doubt it.' Donna smiled. 'Don't lose any sleep over it, Sally. It happens to all of us.'

As she let herself into her room, Sally thought that this had to be one of the worst days of her life. The only bright spot was learning that Fiona was working again. Sally had not mentioned to Donna that she had seen her dancing when she was supposed to be sick. She still wanted to tackle Fiona about it first, when she got the chance.

She went out on to the balcony and leaned

on the rail, looking out over the peaceful village. Perhaps coming here had been a terrible mistake after all. She should have stuck it out in her shop, allowed the past to fade in its own time. Instead she had given up her thriving business for a job which, due to two complaining busybodies, might no longer be hers. She had caught one of her colleagues out in a barefaced lie about being ill, and she had risked everything to tell the man she was falling in love with of her feelings and had only succeeded in alienating him.

Angrily she struck her fist against the balcony rail. Last time she had failed, or so she thought, by not speaking out enough. Paul had driven off and been killed. This time she had voiced her fears in plenty of time, and had again failed. Dean had been angry, and now there seemed no way to cross the gulf that had opened between them.

It was her fault again, she decided. She had mishandled the situation. She knew Dean's unfettered spirits and nature, and should have let him alone. It was no good applying what had happened to Paul to him. And perhaps she had mishandled the Grundeys, too. She might have been able to get on better with them if she'd tried.

Dissatisfied with herself, out of sorts with the world, Sally remained staring into the distance until it grew dark.

CHAPTER EIGHT

'Sally, Donna, I have something to tell you both.' Fiona stood in the doorway to the outside patio at Nicos' taverna, where the other two already sat drinking coffee and eating breakfast. She was nervous, and waited until Donna said, 'What is it? Come in and tell us—it can't be that bad' before she advanced a few paces. But she did not sit down.

'I feel very bad about this,' she began, no trace of her usual good spirits on her face. 'I didn't really want to keep it a secret—but I had to.'

Donna and Sally looked at one another in alarm. 'What's happened?' they asked, each thinking of the worst that could have befallen Fiona.

She could not keep a straight face for long, and could not resist a nervous giggle. 'If you could only see your faces!'

'Please don't keep us in suspense any longer,' commanded Donna. 'Do you need help?'

'That only makes me feel worse,' Fiona said, looking down. She took a deep breath, then announced, 'I'm getting married.'

'But that's wonderful news.'

'Congratulations, that's really great.'

Both Donna and Sally were delighted and

relieved.

'In three weeks' time,' she added.

There was a short silence. 'Wow,' said Donna at last. 'You move fast. No wonder you were worried. But we'll work something out. When do you want to leave—and who is the lucky feller?'

'Oh no, I won't be leaving—at least, not until the end of the summer.'

'He's coming out here? That'll be idyllic—weeks on a Greek island for your honeymoon.' Donna smiled but Sally kept silent, feeling there was more to come.

'No, he won't be coming out here—' the worst over, Fiona's eyes began to twinkle with mischief, and she sat down—'because he already lives here.'

'Fiona, stop teasing, and tell us the whole story, from the beginning.'

'We met last year, and then we wrote to each other like mad during the winter, and when I came back he asked me to marry him. I said yes straight away. I love him, and I want to live here and have a big family.'

'Who *is* it?' demanded Sally, who couldn't wait any longer.

'It's Nicos, of course.'

'Well, you have good taste—but why did it have to be a secret?'

Fiona sighed. 'I knew you wouldn't try to dissuade me. I should have told you before. You see, my parents were dead against us getting married. Every time a letter arrived from Nicos in the winter, they would frown and shake their heads. I've nearly gone mad this summer trying to win them over. And Nicos' parents weren't too happy about an outsider either. That's why I've been taking all this time off work.'

'I suppose your family didn't want to lose you, living so far away. And they won't understand the language either,' said Donna.

'Oh, they understand the language all right. I'm half-Greek myself. Didn't you know?' She shook her dark curls. 'My grandfather came from the Peloponnese, and there are still hundreds of relatives we visit. No, they thought they had escaped from the hard life to live in England, despite the rain. They hated the idea of me going back to scrape a living on an island—all hard work in the summer, and no fun in the winter. But it's what I want.'

*   *   *

Fiona's jaw was set determinedly in her pretty, heart-shaped face.

'And I thought you were Scottish,' Sally said. 'With a name like Fiona.'

'That was my mum. She had a thing about misty Scotland at the time. Thought the country was very romantic after seeing a film about Bonnie Prince Charlie. If I'd been a boy, I'd have been a Charlie!

112

'You do see, I couldn't tell you until it was definite, although Nicos and I went ahead with our plans anyway. I had such a hard time fighting my parents, I didn't want to fight you, too.'

'So you'll get married here in Xora?' Sally asked.

'Yes, and you're both invited, of course. But before that there's a big festival in the mountain village where Nicos' grandfather lives, the head of the family, and we have to be there so that the whole family can be witness to our engagement.'

'Is that Rakion village?' asked Donna. 'I think I've heard about this festival. I wonder if we could take a coach party up there?'

'That's a good idea,' Fiona said excitedly. 'You see I shall also be the festival queen— not much to it, except wearing a crown and smiling a lot. But I was going to ask both of you if you'd be my attendants, or princesses or whatever. My bridesmaids at the actual wedding will be some of Nicos' nieces.'

Sally and Donna exchanged a smile. 'We'd love to do it,' Donna said delightedly. 'But I think a coach party as well might be too much.'

'Oh no, they're so hospitable they'd love it, I'm sure. The more the merrier. I'll ask Nicos about it.'

Sally was doubly pleased to hear Fiona's news. Her secret was out now, and she was obviously radiantly happy—and what's more, at least one of Sally's problems was now resolved. Fiona explained that she had been practising for the festival display dances, which would be done in folk costume. Sally was very relieved she would not have to tackle her after all. She wished her other problems could be so easily resolved.

*   *   *

Sally was sitting alone in a café several days later. Although she had gone about her duties efficiently, time had passed slowly and her heart was heavy. Matching her mood, a torpor hung over the village. Apart from a dog scratching itself in the shade, two people sitting outside a café opposite, and the hum of the big ceiling fan inside, nothing stirred. She was finding it difficult to throw off the sense of failure which still dogged her footsteps, the very thing she had wanted to escape when she came to Greece.

However, as far as her job was concerned, there was still hope. She knew she was good at it now, had settled in, and Donna had sent a favourable report to Sun Sea about Sally. Even Arthur Sims was keeping his distance and not causing any trouble. It had occurred to her that he might have been employed by Sun Sea to spy on her but, if that was the case, he had obviously collected enough evidence to satisfy him on Micro Aspro for he hadn't bothered

114

since.

Of Dean there had been no sign, and hardly a mention of his name. Sally tried hard not to think about him, but failed miserably. When she thought about it, their relationship to date seemed so gossamer thin—and yet it hadn't torn apart, at least not for her. It was a tormenting puzzle.

'Hi—can I join you?'

'Hi, Fiona.' Sally welcomed the interruption. 'Let me get you a drink. How are the wedding plans coming along?'

'Great. My parents will be arriving soon, the dress is ready—it's a family heirloom from Nicos' grandmother, altered to fit—and Nicos is threatening to run away.'

'Is he that nervous?'

'Yes, but apparently it's normal. Even I'm wondering if I've made a terrible mistake. Do you think I should call the whole thing off?'

Smiling, Sally shook her head. 'It's just last-minute nerves, isn't it?'

'I suppose so. I wish it was all over, including the festival in Rakion—all those disapproving relatives. That reminds me, the SunSea trip is on if anyone wants to go.' She stopped. 'Don't I know him?'

'Oh, yes,' said Sally, following the direction of her eyes. 'That's Peter Elsing—and he's seen us.'

'Sally—you've been hiding from me. How are you?' He pulled up a chair and sat down to join them.

'I'm fine, Peter. This is Fiona. She works for SunSea, too.'

'And I'm just about to get married,' Fiona told him. 'We're going to have one of the most unusual engagement parties ever—we were just talking about it.'

'I hope I'm going to be invited,' Peter said, clearly taking to Fiona. 'Who's the lucky man?'

'Nicos—he owns the taverna up the top there. And of course you can come to the party, anyone can. Open house at the Rakion Festival, they say.'

'Rakion! I was going there anyway. I'm looking forward to seeing the costume dances,' Peter said enthusiastically, before giving his order to the waiter who had come over. Sally remembered his mentioning it over their lunch.

'Fiona's been practising,' Sally said. 'But then, she's going to be the most important woman there, and everyone will be watching her.'

'Yes, and I'm terrified I'll make a mistake.'

'Are you going too, Sally?'

'Donna and I are going to be Fiona's ladies-in-waiting! But I don't expect we shall be doing any dancing.'

'Oh, you must. It's very important that you should. You see, the festival dates from prehistoric times—no, don't groan. You may as well know the reason for it. Kouros always

116

has these freak summer storms, so they would hold a big festival for the sea god to propitiate him. He was supposed to have especially enjoyed the dances.'

'Now the priest blesses the sea,' Fiona joined in. 'It's become a Christian festival, but for the same purpose. Then, afterwards, there won't be any more storms till the autumn.'

'Well, if your friend Donna is as ravishing as you two, I'm sure the sight of your dancing would please anyone, let alone mere mortal men,' said Peter.

*   *   *

Sally gave a wry smile. Peter's flattery was sincere and well meant, she could see, and now they were all talking in such an open and friendly fashion, she wondered if the strangeness she had attributed to him at his hotel had been imaginary.

'I'm glad there'll be someone else on my side in Rakion anyway,' Fiona was saying.

'Of course. And I'll be bringing along the film director and a couple of the boys, too. They'll love it. They'll be here in two days' time—you haven't forgotten the party, have you, Sally?'

'Oh—no. That's very kind of you. How about it, Fiona?'

'Um, well I'd like to, but Nicos and I have such a lot to do. Speak of the devil, there he is.

Won't be a moment.'

Fiona and Nicos stood talking together in the hot street, their eyes shining with love and tenderness. Sally looked away hastily, and found Peter observing her.

'You're looking a bit down,' he said. 'The party will cheer you up.'

'I'll have to talk to Donna about it.' Sally sought for an excuse. She didn't feel like socialising at all. 'Make sure there's nothing official on for that night.'

'OK. I hope you'll be free. By the way, I'm glad we've got this moment alone. I want to apologise for boring—and perhaps frightening you—a little bit the other day. I've got rid of those objects now, as you said I should.'

'I expect that's for the best. How is your article coming along?'

'Very well, I'll have finished it soon. Then, with the film work mainly done too, I should have more free time. Perhaps I'll be able to see more of you.'

Sally murmured something noncommittal. As long as Peter kept his distance, she wouldn't mind seeing him from time to time.

*   *   *

Theopolis was busy, noisy and dirty. Donna had asked Sally to go in to fetch some medical supplies from the main pharmacy, as their first-aid stocks were low. Sally had not minded.

Just lately Xora had become claustrophobic, and she was glad to get away.

When she had completed her purchases, she had two hours' wait for the next bus back to Xora—they only ran three times a day. She knew she could take a taxi, but decided that this provided a perfect opportunity to explore further the alleyways of the old part of the town.

She strolled through the lively streets, feeling her spirits lift as she absorbed the sights and sounds around her. It was while she was looking at a display of sponges that she thought she caught sight, out of the corner of her eye, of a familiar figure. She dropped the sponge and, ignoring the pleas of the old shopkeeper, who thought he'd made a sale, hurried after the figure, almost without thinking.

She stopped outside the shop into which she'd seen Dean—or someone who looked very like him—disappear. Her heart thudding, she was about to make herself walk on by— after all, what was she doing, chasing him about?—when a quick glance through the window revealed Dean looking out at her. A look of mingled surprise, annoyance and pleasure shot across his face. He had been talking to a swarthy, middle-aged man in tinted glasses, but broke off the conversation and came to the door where Sally was rooted to the spot.

'Sally, what are you doing here? Were you looking for me?'

'Not especially. It was just a coincidence. I've been shopping again.' She held up her purchases to show him. She saw him hesitate, and expected him to tell her to leave him alone. She tensed herself ready for a rebuff which did not come.

'I won't be long,' he said. 'Wait for me here.'

He ducked back into the shop where the proprietor, who had been watching their exchange with ill-concealed irritation, immediately began an impassioned speech, waving his hand for emphasis. Sally noticed that the shop sold rocks and quartzes, and not particularly pretty ones at that.

'You speak Greek very well,' Sally said admiringly when Dean re-emerged.

'I speak terrible Greek, but enough to get by. But surely you can tell that?'

'Oh, no—I can just about decipher the alphabet, and read a little, and I've learned key phrases from the guide book. But I can't understand a Greek person when they're talking.'

Dean laughed, seeming to relax. 'Half the time, neither can I.' And the tight sensation in her stomach relaxed. 'We'll go to a bar I know, where it's quiet. Stay close or you'll get lost in all these people.'

*   *   *

Dean dived off through the close-packed strolling crowds and Sally had to hurry to keep up with him. Fortunately his height made him stand out, so that she could not lose sight of him. He was wearing jeans as usual, and a loose short-sleeved white shirt. His rich brown hair was attractively lightened by the sun.

Suddenly he turned under an archway and Sally found they were in a quiet courtyard where a fountain splashed intermittently. Under a colonnade to one side was an open-fronted bar. One other person was sitting on the high bar stool; preoccupied with his drink, he only glanced briefly in their direction.

The stony-faced barman brought their drinks, and pushed a bowl of nuts in their direction.

'So,' Dean began, 'you came souvenir-shopping to Theopolis.'

'No, I came for medical supplies, then decided to look around. I love this part of the town—and I'm so glad I bumped into you,' Sally said quietly.

'I'm glad you did too,' he said. 'I've been thinking about you, and I'm sorry we parted the way we did.'

'That's just what I—'

'But you needn't have stormed off like that.'

'Me!' Sally fought hard to hold on to her good intentions. 'After what you said, what did you expect?'

Dean smiled wryly. 'I suppose I should thank you for keeping your suspicions to yourself, at least.'

'My suspicions? Are you suffering from hurt pride? I didn't mean to sound as if I thought you were a criminal, and I'm sorry if I did. That's why I'm glad to see you. I've wanted to apologise,' Sally said hotly, not sounding in the least contrite.

'That's OK. I can take it. My pride isn't as insufferable as you seem to think it is. But don't you think you gave up too easily? If you'd stayed around, who knows what you might have found out.'

Sally rose to the challenge. 'I didn't want to find out anything. You misunderstood me,' she said in frustration. 'I only offered to help—but perhaps that's what galled you.'

'If I need help I'll ask for it. I don't, so you're wasting your time.'

'Oh, I give in,' Sally said, thumping her clenched fists against her knees. 'We're back just where we started, arguing at cross purposes. I still don't know what I've said to annoy you. I think we should call it a day. Thanks for the drink—and maybe I'll see you around.'

She jumped down from the stool and without a backward glance made her way across the open courtyard. The other man at the bar did not even look up from his newspaper as she went and she was relieved;

she felt as if she'd made a spectacle of herself. But she was hurt, and wanted to get away. What had got into Dean that he both refused to come clean to her, or to back down?

As she passed under the archway towards the busy street, a strong hand gripped her from behind.

'Dammit, Sally, you can't go like this.' Dean pulled her back towards him, turning her round and pinioning her arms at her sides. 'Dammit,' he said again, then pressed his mouth against her willing lips, holding her tight against him in the shadow of the arch, oblivious of the curious glances of passers-by.

'Hey,' Dean said, releasing her a little, 'we should do this more often. It's more pleasurable than fighting.'

'Oh, Dean,' Sally said, pressing her face against his chest and closing her eyes, relishing his nearness. 'I don't want to argue. And what was it about anyway?'

'I don't know. I've forgotten already, and I'm sure it doesn't matter. Now come on back and finish your drink, and we'll talk about something else.'

Arms around each other's waists, they strolled companionably back to the bar, where the barman acknowledged their return with an impassive, world-weary lift of his eyebrow.

*   *   *

'You're looking fantastic tonight, Sally. Where are you off to?' Donna asked, as they met each other by chance in the street in Xora.

'I'm meeting Dean. We ran across each other in Theopolis a couple of days ago and we've arranged to spend the evening together.'

Donna surveyed the flush in Sally's cheek beneath the golden tan, the sparkle in her clear, light blue eyes, the half-smile on her parted lips. 'You and Dean are getting pretty close then?' she asked smilingly.

'We seem to have buried our differences for now, yes.'

'Every couple has tiffs—or most do. You should have heard me and Colin in the early days.'

'Thanks, I'll remember that. What do you think of my dress, by the way?' She twirled to show off the dress, white shot with silver thread, which she had bought for herself in Xora.

'It's lovely, and I'm hideously jealous. I've been admiring it in the shop window myself—but I must dash. Have a lovely evening.'

'And you.' Sally continued on her way to the main square, humming to herself. It was early evening, a faint pink flush in the darkening sky. A few stars had appeared, vying with the brilliant silver disc of the full moon, and the air smelled fresh and exciting.

Yes, she and Dean had resolved their differences. At least, in her case she had

124

determined to live day-by-day, and enjoy his company as and when she could. If he said no strings, no prying, then at the moment she felt she could cope with that. She steadfastly refused to think of tomorrow—after all, the romantic bubble could so easily burst. For now, she was going to try it his way.

She sat down at an outside table, exchanged a few words with the bar owner who brought her a cool drink, and waited for Dean to arrive. When she saw him, striding confidently through the strolling holidaymakers, she felt her heart give its accustomed leap at the sight of him, and the faces around him became a blur—all, that is, except one.

Dean and Peter Elsing reached her at the same time. As soon as she recognised Peter, her heart dropped. He spoke first.

'Hello, Sally. All dressed up and ready to go, eh? Perhaps you'd like something to eat first before the party?'

Sally looked helplessly at Dean, but he remained expressionless, not helping her out. 'Party?' she repeated stupidly. 'I don't—'

'The film party, of course. But I thought that's why you were waiting here for me. Don't say you'd forgotten.'

'Oh no—I *had* forgotten. Peter, I'm sorry, but—'

'What Sally's trying to say is that we're both looking forward to the party. Isn't that right, honey?' Dean cut in swiftly, clearly enjoying the look of disappointment on Peter's face.

'But, Dean, we don't have to go.'

'Oh, but we do. You promised Peter here, and we can't let him down.'

Dean's eyes were glittering, but Sally knew it wasn't with laughter. She turned to Peter. 'You've met Dean before, haven't you? Are you sure it'll be all right—for both of us to come?'

'Yes, I'm sure that'll be OK. The more the merrier,' he said with false heartiness. 'Shall we go and get a meal now?'

'Dean—it's a mistake,' Sally hissed as soon as Peter was out of earshot. 'I never promised I'd go to the stupid party—I forgot all about it. He asked all three of us.'

'Sure you did, but it's not an opportunity to miss, is it? See how the other half live. We'll have a great time. I'm looking forward to it.'

*   *   *

Sally subsided into silence at his side. His words were perfectly bland, but she could tell from his tone that he didn't believe her.

Under any other circumstances, the party would have been highly enjoyable. The film crew was a small team, as yet, the advance guard. None of the actors and actresses had arrived and so the party was informal and jolly. There were a few Greeks present whom Peter thought would be useful contacts, too.

126

Dean was soon drawn into conversation, and Sally found herself chatting with the director's assistant. But every now and then, when she looked across at Dean, she felt that his answering gaze was more of a glower. Why wouldn't he believe her about the mix-up? If only he would come out with it and clear the air. Her hopes for a wonderful evening were utterly dashed.

She made sure that she never spoke to Peter alone, and he, to give him his due, did not single her out either, which was something to be thankful for.

Dean and Sally left some time after midnight and walked hand-in-hand through the streets, deserted except for a few late-night revellers.

'I had no idea Peter would find me,' Sally began again. 'I'm sorry our plans were spoiled.'

Dean squeezed her hand. 'No need to keep saying you're sorry. I enjoyed myself. Didn't you?'

'Not very much,' Sally confessed. 'I was thinking of you.'

'Then you shouldn't have been. You've got to throw off your guilt—you had as much right to a good time as I did.'

Sally's heart plummeted. She should welcome his uncomplicated attitude, she knew—if only she didn't feel him secretly seething underneath his careless facade.

They discussed the party inconsequentially,

then, outside Sofia's house, Dean stopped. 'This is where I leave you,' he said. He pulled her into his arms and kissed her roughly, bruising her lips, his eyes wide open and staring into hers.

'Remember, Sally, trust is the name of the game.' And with that cryptic statement, he left her.

Sadly, she climbed the stairs to her room. Star-crossed lovers was putting it mildly. Just about everything that could go wrong, had. But she did trust Dean, despite herself. After all, she was madly in love with him.

CHAPTER NINE

The road to Rakion wound tortuously up the side of the valley.

The SunSea coach had to manoeuvre carefully, almost getting stuck on the final bend before the village. The party left the coach at the first sign of houses and continued on foot. Most of the single-storey houses they passed were in need of a fresh coat of white paint, and scrawny cats and dogs roamed the main street where children, dressed in their best clothes, ran screaming and shouting in play. There was no road out of Rakion, it simply turned into a path that led over rough mountain terrain suitable only for sheep and goats.

It was early evening. The sun had just set, and the evening stars shone faintly in the pale sky. It seemed that all the inhabitants were out of doors, the men in carefully mended and pressed shirts and trousers, the women in pretty summer dresses. Fiona told Sally that many of the people they saw did not live in the village, but had returned to visit their families there for the festival.

There was an atmosphere of subdued excitement. As the English group progressed along the narrow street, the Greek people shook their hands and welcomed them, calling 'Hello' in English.

The feast was to be held in the main square. Tables had already been set out in long rows, and covered with checked paper tablecloths. Above them, fairylights criss-crossed the open space. One table was separated from the others.

While the tourists wandered around the village, making friends and taking pictures, Fiona led Sally and Donna across to Nicos, who was standing with an old man wearing a dark brown suit, wrinkled with age. The old man lifted his hat, and Nicos introduced him. 'My grandfather.'

When he smiled, he revealed more gaps than teeth, but when he spoke his voice was still strong, and his handshake was firm.

'He says you are very welcome,' Nicos

interpreted. 'And that you are both very beautiful. He hopes you will be happy tonight, then everyone can be happy. You know, there is a saying that when the festival queen and her princesses smile, only good will come to Rakion.'

'We certainly hope so,' said Donna, while Sally smiled at the old man who seemed very taken with her. 'Is there anything special we have to do, apart from smile?'

'You will sit there—' Nicos pointed to the table set apart—'and one of you will be first to dance—with my grandfather. Don't worry, he will do all the dancing, you will see. Then Fiona and I will dance, and after that—the world goes crazy.'

While Donna remained with Nicos and his grandfather, Fiona put her arm through Sally's and drew her away to meet Nicos' grandmother, a whiskery old woman in dark blue, sitting on a wooden chair outside her home. They nodded and smiled to one another while Fiona explained who Sally was.

'She says she likes your dress very much. Very pretty.'

'Thanks—I wasn't sure what I should wear, and I'm glad it's suitable.' She had chosen the same white dress she had worn to the party a few days before. Her shoes had low heels, and she had put her hair up into a French plait. Gold drop earrings and a plain gold chain around her neck were her only jewellery. She was conscious of the contrast between the dark good looks around her, and her own pallor.

'They're not quite as old as they look,' Fiona explained as they walked away. 'They say that you grow older faster in Rakion because you are too near the sun here. It's the highest village on Kouros and every summer, when the storms come, there's nearly always a sheep or goat killed by lightning.'

'Was that one of them over there?' asked Sally, pointing to where meat was being spit roasted over an open fire in a brick hearth.

'No, that was probably killed today, with special blessings and old proverbs. There are more being cooked inside the bigger houses, too, and the Kafenion chap will be bringing out salads and bread.'

There was plenty of mouth-watering meat to go round, even though it arrived in haphazard fashion. Once everyone was seated, the meat was passed on plates, and the bread in baskets, from hand to hand until most people had something in front of them, and what they didn't have, they shared with a neighbour. Bottles of Rakion wine and jugs of water were passed around, too.

*   *   *

It was quite dark, the lights from the houses surrounding the square and the fairylights above providing enough illumination to eat by. A myriad of stars glistened in the night sky, and the noisy talk and laughter drifted from the village across the valley below, as it had done for thousands of years. In defiance of the gods who sent the storms, Sally thought. Dean and Peter were both quite right. You could get interested in olden times in the right setting.

But she didn't want to think of either man. Tonight she was determined to leave her troubles far below in Xora. She smiled across at Donna, flame-like in her red dress, her rich curling hair cascading over her shoulders. Fiona glowed in blue, her glossy black hair pinned up in curls on top of her head. Donna's 'crown' of flowers had been set at a rakish angle by one of the men in a mischievous moment; Sally felt incredibly lucky to work with such nice people.

Tonight, surrounded by the goodwill and high spirits of the people of Rakion, she could take pleasure in Fiona's happiness. It was her night, and nothing could spoil it. Sally no longer regretted her decision to come to Greece. She had learned so much, had come to love Greece and its people. It was a pity Dean had to come along and muddy the waters.

Nicos' grandfather pushed back his chair and stood up, and gradually a hush of sorts fell. His speech, sadly none of which Sally understood, was short, causing a roar of laughter from the villagers. There was much clapping and clinking of glasses as people linked arms with their neighbours to drink a toast. The old man now gestured for Sally to stand up as two men came forward and struck up a tune, one on a battered accordion, the other on a violin.

'Good luck,' called Donna. 'I'm glad he didn't choose me!'

Sally found all she had to do was stand on one spot, sway a little and clap as the old man, with great agility, capered around her, sometimes touching the ground with his hands, or slapping his heels. She clapped and laughed her appreciation of his skill.

Fiona and Nicos came out, too, then others, some in costume. The old man, honour satisfied, retired to one side, but Sally was expected to continue. As she was whirled through several dances, she waved to the SunSea holidaymakers, who were evidently having a great time—apart, that is, from Arthur Sims who sat with a small grimace on his mouth a little way from the others. She saw, too, that Peter Elsing had come, as he said he would. He was sitting with three people whom she recognised from the party a few nights before.

Suddenly struck by sharp sadness at the memory of Dean, Sally was relieved when the music stopped momentarily and the costumed dancers assembled to perform a special Rakion folk dance. Sally took the opportunity to slip away and catch her breath. She felt her head spinning from the local wine, and decided to take a short stroll to recover her equilibrium.

She left the noisy square behind her, and walked along a dark and deserted street, the houses on either side shuttered up. A dog howled, and was answered by another. The moon, now beginning to wane, threw a strong light which sharpened the shadows and made them thicker, blacker. The cool air was refreshing to Sally's cheeks, and she deliberately blanked her mind out as she walked, recovering from the wave of pain she had felt at the thought of Dean.

After a few minutes she discovered she had come to the end of the village. The last house was tiny, little bigger than a chicken shack, and the bare open grazing land of the mountain lay ahead, interrupted by small clumps of low-growing shrubs. As she was about to turn back, however, she thought she heard something.

Yes, there it was again. Indistinct voices, not far away. She looked around and decided they must be coming from behind some rocks. She took two paces forward then halted. It was none of her business, and yet there had been something familiar about one of the voices. Cautiously, she picked her way over the rough ground towards the rocks. Now she could hear more clearly. A low, muttering voice and then—yes, surely that had been Dean's voice replying, unless it was simply that she had been thinking about him. He seemed to be speaking Greek, but she thought she'd recognise his tone anywhere, let alone his American accent.

*　　　*　　　*

Curiosity overcame her better judgment and she crept on, reached the rocks, and then edged her way around. She stopped, pressing herself against the sharp contours of the weathered stone.

On the other side, the ground dipped sharply away and in the hollow stood three men. She could see them clearly in the moonlight. Dean stood in the centre, facing a tall, thin man who was speaking fast, waving his arms. To one side, and a little behind Dean, stood the other Greek, fatter and thickset. Sally recognised him. He was the owner of the shop in Xora where she had seen the coins displayed at such a high price; where Peter Elsing had found her that time.

What on earth was Dean doing here? she wondered. And what would he say if he ever found out she had spied on him? But as she watched she saw the thin man make a threatening lunge, forcing Dean to step back. All at once she realised that this was no ordinary conversation taking place. Dean was arguing, shaking his head vehemently. Even though she cursed herself for not being able

135

to follow the Greek language, there was no mistaking his emphatic 'No!'.

So he was refusing to do or say something—but how serious was the trouble he was in, and had he deserved it? Sally dismissed the thought immediately. Whatever it was, she knew she wanted no harm to come to him. He'd been a fool to come here in the first place, and she berated him in her mind for taking such a stupid risk.

She snapped upright. The thin man had grabbed Dean's arm, and they tussled together for a second while Sally held her breath, then Dean broke free but held his ground.

She was in a desperate quandary now. She wanted to fetch help—there was no point in her interfering directly, she'd only complicate matters. But Dean had made it clear that he would not welcome her aid. He might not thank her if she summoned men from the village.

As she tried to resolve the dilemma, concentrating on the scene below, she was suddenly seized from behind and a hand clamped over her mouth.

'Well, Sally,' a voice said softly in her ear. 'I've been wanting to get close to you, but I didn't expect it to be in circumstances like these.'

Peter Elsing's body was pressed close against hers as he held her with one arm around her waist. She had not realised he had such strength in his wiry frame. She shook her head violently to free herself from his hand, but to no avail. As they struggled, Peter threw her off-balance and she slammed against the rock.

She felt nauseated by the blow and by his closeness, and shut her eyes briefly to try to clear her head.

'That's it, Sally, lie still and I promise no harm will come to you—yet, anyway,' Peter murmured. 'And then we'll find out exactly what you're doing here.'

We? Sally thought Peter must somehow be involved in the scene taking place below, and it seemed that the odds against Dean were building up. She opened her eyes again to see Dean grappling with the tall man. He stepped backwards, his arm drawn back ready to punch. Under Sally's horrified gaze, the fat shop owner took an object from his pocket and barked a command. The moonlight glinted off the barrel of a snub-nosed automatic. But Dean was already moving forward as the click of the safety catch being removed rang through the clear night air.

*　　　*　　　*

Sally felt Peter stiffen in anticipation behind her, and did not stop to think. She bit his hand full square, with all her might. As, with a startled gasp, he relaxed his grip, she yelled

137

at the top of her voice. 'Dean, look behind—' before Peter viciously tightened his grip and covered her mouth again, cursing her.

Too late. A shot rang out, and Dean was hurled to the ground by the force of the bullet. The other two men spun in her direction and Peter called out to them.

The world tilted crazily. Dean was shot! But he couldn't be dead. She wouldn't let him be.

'Lover boy's done for now. You'd better come in with me,' Peter said, triumph in his voice. Sally kicked at his shins and felt triumphant contact.

When she looked down, she saw that Dean was moving, trying to struggle to his knees. The relief was so great that her legs turned to jelly, and she hardly felt the stinging slap Peter delivered to her face. But even as she slumped gratefully against the rock, the two men were closing in on Dean and she knew she could do nothing to help him.

Then another voice rang out and, to her utter disbelief—and Peter's too, judging by his sharp intake of breath—Arthur Sims appeared on the other side of the hollow. He was minus his hat but it was definitely Arthur Sims, a changed Arthur Sims. He seemed somehow taller, the sour expression gone from his face to leave a taut authoritative expression. He, too, was holding a gun.

Peter swore again. 'It was you, wasn't it, who tipped him off? I should have guessed, but you took me right in, you little pest.'

Sally tried to shake her head, making noises in her throat, but Peter went on, 'Still, perhaps you can be useful to me after all. You'll be my passage to freedom.' And he began to hurry her away on trembling legs, leaving her with a confused image of other people coming up beside Arthur Sims, and Dean staggering to his feet.

Sally did all she could to hinder their progress over the uneven ground. From what Peter had said she was sure that Arthur Sims was not a welcome sight, and that Dean was safe now. Unless, that is—but she didn't have time to straighten her muddled thoughts about who was on who's side, and who was in the right, for Peter suddenly released his grip on her and she stumbled, almost falling, saving herself just in time.

Two uniformed men were now holding Peter, who was making no effort to free himself, his head hanging sullenly. They spoke to her in Greek and she had to say 'I don't understand' before addressing Peter.

'Peter, what the hell's been going on? What have you done, and why—'

'No need to play the innocent any longer,' he spat at her. 'I should have known, you being so thick with the American, but I thought you were out of it. Sammy will kill me for this,' he added desperately.

'Who's Sammy?' Sally demanded, but Peter

refused to answer and the two policemen were now propelling him back the way they had come, towards the hollow. Sally followed on shaking legs. She half-dreaded what might be awaiting her. She had seen Dean stand up, but he was a powerful man. Supposing the bullet had . . . Her hands were icy cold and perspiration started from her pores.

They circled the rocks, clambering downwards, and in the clearing stood Dean, clasping one shoulder but otherwise unharmed. By his side stood Arthur Sims. Two policemen had handcuffed the other Greeks, and Sally saw Arthur Sims casually open his jacket and replace his gun in his shoulder holster.

'Dean,' she said, her voice a croak.

'Sally—oh, Sally—I knew it was you.' He came towards her, arm outstretched. Thankfully, she clung to him, trying to avoid his wounded shoulder.

'I think you saved my life,' Dean murmured. 'I don't know what you're doing here, and I don't care. But when you called out I looked round and moved my position. The shot got me in the shoulder. It was meant for my heart, I'm sure.' To her annoyance Sally felt tears gathering in her eyes and a lump welling in her throat.

'You're safe,' she managed to say. 'When you fell, I didn't know—I mean, you moved, but—'

'Hush, my darling,' Dean said, stroking her face then kissing away her tears. 'Everything's all right.'

There was a light cough behind them, and Arthur Sims said, 'Everything might not be all right if we don't get this young man to a doctor soon. He is losing blood.'

'Of course,' Sally gasped, seeing for the first time that Dean's shirt was soaked with his blood. It had stained her clothes too.

'Your dress,' Dean said. 'It's ruined.'

'I don't care—do you want me to tear it up for bandages?'

Dean grinned. 'Now she's Florence Nightingale—' He closed his eyes and swayed.

'As I said, a doctor. The reaction's setting in. Come on, Sally, you take his other arm,' Arthur Sims directed. Together, they supported Dean as they made their way back towards the village in the wake of the police and their three charges.

'Mr. Sims,' Sally began. 'Just who exactly are you? You seem so different from when you arrived on Kouros.'

He chuckled. 'I don't enjoy adopting obnoxious disguises, but you must admit you'd never have guessed I'm from Interpol.'

'No never! We—I mean I—thought you were a peeping tom.'

'I thought you were acting distinctly suspiciously,' said Dean.

'Save your breath, young man,' Arthur

Sims said severely. 'Yes, a poor piece of eavesdropping on my part, there. You didn't rumble me though, thank goodness.'

'So can you both tell me what it's all about now?' Sally asked.

'For one thing, when I saw that both you and Peter Elsing were gone this evening, I thought I'd better find out what you were up to. I was sure by then that you, Sally, were only an innocent bystander, but Elsing's another matter. He's the reason I came to Kouros in the first place.'

Sally cast a glance in Dean's direction. He avoided meeting her eye.

'I am quite innocent,' she affirmed. 'But I still don't know why you are here. What was Peter doing?'

'Smuggling ancient Greek artefacts. I've been following the trail from England.'

'But he told me he was a lecturer.'

'So he is. He just dabbles on the side.'

'Were they trying to make them join you, Dean?' she asked.

He laughed weakly. 'I'm an archaeologist—the dig is near the beach.'

Sally was silent, absorbing this startling revelation. 'But why didn't you—' she began, when Arthur Sims broke in: 'Mr. Samuelson was put under pressure to allow some of the items he found to fall into the wrong hands.'

'I see,' Sally murmured, and tightened her grip around Dean's waist. There was a lot of explaining to do, but that could come later. For now, all that mattered was that Dean was alive, and he'd called her his darling.

CHAPTER TEN

The little church of St. Theodosius stood only a short distance from the beach, across grass long since scorched colourless by the sun. The sea breezes did not penetrate that far. Inside, the richly decorated church was hot and stuffy. As many people as possible had squeezed inside to witness Nicos and Fiona's wedding, friends and family occupying the few benches at the front, everyone else standing behind. Beside an ornate brass lectern and draped altar stood the priest in his black robes and square black hat.

Sally and Donna were standing behind the immediate family. Sally had admired the glowing paintings on the walls, their rich reds and blues finished off in gold leaf. When she had stepped into the church earlier, she had felt as if she was passing into a different world.

The wedding procession had been waved on by well-wishers, villagers and tourists alike, for news of the wedding had spread fast. Nicos, in his best suit, gazed fixedly ahead, obviously nervous, his straight black hair gleaming. Fiona was resplendent in a white satin dress, slightly yellowed with age, and a long lace veil. She had given Sally and Donna a wink from beneath the gauze as she passed by.

The deep, sonorous intonation of the priest contrasted with the quiet answers of Fiona and Nicos as the solemnisation of their marriage proceeded, and Sally realised that she felt at peace for the first time in long weeks. She closed her eyes for a moment, feeling great gratitude that she and Dean were safe now, unharmed apart from the bullet that had passed cleanly through the flesh of Dean's shoulder.

When she opened her eyes, Nicos and Fiona were kneeling, holding hands, and they looked at one another so sweetly that a tear moistened the corner of her eye. She and Donna smiled at one another.

'I'm so happy for them,' whispered Donna. 'Don't they look lovely together?'

'Yes. I hope everything works out well for them,' Sally whispered back.

Now the young couple were walking hand in hand down the aisle, and the small crowd surged after them into the sunshine. Outside, flowers and sweets were thrown, and benedictions called for health and happiness.

'Went all right, didn't it?' said Fiona matter-of-factly to them, before being whisked away to be hugged by Nicos' mother, and then by her own, while her father shook Nicos' hand. There was no sign now of their opposition to the marriage, and both families walked amicably together back to the village while Sally and Donna followed behind.

*   *   *

The wedding feast was being held out of doors, in a large garden behind one of the tavernas, redolent with the scents of roses and jasmine. The food was laid out on white cloth-covered tables, and there were many delicacies Sally had not seen before.

'Let's get a table over there, under that tree,' said Donna, gripping her elbow and propelling her through the crowd. 'Then we can save a seat for Dean. He is coming, isn't he?'

'As soon as the doctor has finished checking his wound. He hoped to be here already.'

Donna shuddered. 'When I think what you two went through that night . . . And you've hardly had a chance to see each other since.'

'You had a bad time too, Fiona told me, when you discovered I'd vanished.'

'I was so ashamed I hadn't noticed you'd gone earlier.'

'It can only have been a short while, and Arthur Sims was keeping an eye on me anyway,' Sally said as they sat down. They had had this conversation several times already, but Donna still felt responsible.

A waiter brought them a selection of meats

145

and pastries, and a bottle of wine, then Donna continued, 'That Peter Elsing was a real snake in the grass, wasn't he? Do you think he was planning to use you in some way?'

Sally sighed. 'I don't know, possibly. Do you know what I found out? When we first met, at the disco, things were just as he said they were—he was lonely. Then, when Dean came over, Peter decided to check me out, to see why we were friendly. He stole a coin from my room which Dean had given me. But he couldn't find anything to tie me in with the police, so he got to know me to keep tabs on me.'

'Ugh.' Donna shuddered. 'Although I think he liked you, too.'

'With friends like that who needs . . . Mmm, try one of these sausages. They're delicious.'

'Thanks. But are you quite recovered now?'

'Oh, yes. Not much to recover from, really.' Sally smiled. 'Dean's the one with the wound.'

Fiona's father stood up to make a toast and a speech, English fashion, and then small children came running round with gifts for everyone before the newly wedded couple began to move from table to table to thank everyone for coming. Nicos' grandfather and other members of his family from Rakion were sitting nearby, and had waved to Donna and Sally.

Then Dean arrived. He stopped to congratulate Nicos and Fiona, then came straight over. 'You both look beautiful,' he said, kissing each of them on the cheek.

'Have some wine and tell us what the doctor said,' ordered Donna, handing him a glass.

'Thanks. He took off the dressing, pronounced me fit, and prescribed a great deal of swimming and sunbathing in the company of the girl of my choice.' He looked at Sally. 'How about it?'

'You bet—I'll keep you to that.'

'Have you finished with the police now?' asked Donna.

'More or less. The big disappointment is that, although they have Elsing and the two Greeks, Sammy and Yorgos, the main European connection has slipped through their fingers yet again.'

'Well, I think you were very brave, standing up to them,' said Donna.

'I did know, before I came here, that something like this was likely to happen. Various items on the black market had been traced back to the dig at Kouros, which is a particularly rich one. That's why I was so particular about keeping the place well guarded, safe from prying eyes.'

He and Sally exchanged a smile, remembering how they had first met.

'I also made sure my team was hand picked and trustworthy.'

'Do you recall telling me how Dean was attacked in Theopolis? That was the same

147

people trying to frighten him into doing as they wanted. And we were followed once, only Dean told me it was the police.'

'I thought if you knew who it really was, you'd be twice as frightened.'

'You managed to hide the fact that you were an archaeologist without any bother. I thought you'd made a million on Wall Street and retired early!' Donna teased.

'I thought it was safer to keep a low profile, and the SunSea trips on the *Dolphin* helped a great deal in that respect.'

'I haven't told you before, Donna, but Dean thought *I* might be tied in with the smugglers. Can you believe that?' Sally grinned, and Dean had the grace to look shamefaced.

'Dean—how could you. You've only got to look at Sally to know it couldn't be true,' Donna said.

'Ah, but that was the trouble.' He leaned forward and took Sally's hand, his hazel eyes glistening mischievously. 'I didn't know if I could trust my instincts. When I found her on that beach—no one had been near there all summer. Then the coin went missing. Was she telling me the truth, in which case I should be worried for her, or had she passed it on? Then, finally, when I had persuaded myself—and Simon, too—that it was really me she was interested in, not what I was digging up, she so carefully arranged for us to go to that party with Elsing who I knew to be in on the smuggling racket. I didn't know what to believe then.'

'You were so angry, but you wouldn't come out and say why.'

'I was angry with myself for having been duped,' Dean told her, and raised her hand to his lips to kiss it.

'You know now he only chatted me up to find out what I was up to!'

Donna poured some more wine for them all. 'There's only one thing I don't understand: why that night, of all nights, to force you to give them what they wanted? And why did you go up there to meet them?'

Dean twirled his wine glass, staring into it meditatively. 'I was given a message that they were holding Sally. Simon told me not to go, that it was a trap, but I couldn't take that chance.'

'You never told me!' Sally gasped.

'How romantic. You went to save Sally,' said Donna, misty-eyed. 'I wonder if Colin would do the same for me?'

'Of course he would. And they chose that particular night because the whole village of Rakion would be occupied with the festival. There are some caves near there which they've used to store their goods.'

'Well, between the two of you, you've ensured that those old treasures will remain here on Kouros.' And Donna held up her glass to them.

'I'll drink to that!' Sally and Dean said together.

*　　*　　*

In the weeks that followed the wedding, Dean acted on his doctor's advice, and he and Sally spent all their free time together. They explored Kouros thoroughly, both up in the mountains, where the villagers rarely saw tourists, and all along the rocky bays with their enticing sandy beaches. They went sailing on the *Dolphin* too, with Sally acting as extra 'crew', slowly learning the rudiments of sailing. She began to understand just how much Dean loved the yacht and his mastery of the sea.

Dean also took Sally to see the dig he was conducting, although he seemed reluctant to take her there often. She decided he probably liked to get right away from his work in his spare time. They walked through the big gates bearing the sign forbidding entry, followed the track for about ten minutes, then came on a busy scene. The excavations were spread over a small area as yet, about an acre, and after many months of painstaking work there was not a great deal to see to Sally's inexperienced eye. The stones that Dean pointed out as marking a shop's boundaries looked to Sally like a pile of old stones.

Simon awarded Sally a dazzling smile of greeting, for now his suspicions of her were allayed.

'You can see there,' Dean pointed out, 'the outline of a big villa. So you see I wasn't lying to you when I said I was building a villa—but perhaps I should have said rebuilding.'

Sally was intrigued to discover a carving of the same face that had been on the stolen coin. 'He looks so friendly, don't you think?' she said. 'I don't know why the people of Kouros once thought he sent storms to devastate them.'

'Yes, especially as the latest storms caused a landslip over there.' Dean pointed to a particularly shapeless pile of mud and rock. 'Which revealed a cache of several urns, all filled with coins. Yorgos, the shop owner, got to hear of this. He managed to bribe one of my helpers, who had since been dismissed. It made him all the more eager to put pressure on me. There would have been a huge profit in it for him if he'd got hold of even half of these. When I wouldn't play, though, he thought the best thing was to get rid of me. Someone new might have been easier to deal with.'

Simon, standing near them, made a noise in his throat and covered his eyes to show his horror of this. Sally smiled. It was a delight to find the sullen scowls gone, and a normal, carefree teenage boy in their place.

Sally would have liked to go back to the site more than the twice Dean took her, but whenever she suggested it he always shook his head and they went to the beach instead.

In September the days grew balmier, the nights cooler. But it was as hot as ever on the beach, and the sea still as warm. Dean and Sally lay side by side on the sand, in the very place which he had ordered her to leave and which they now called 'their' beach. The scar on his shoulder was a pale area of puckered flesh, healing nicely.

Sally drew in a deep breath of contentment. She knew now that whatever had happened in the past was well behind her. Paul's death had been one of life's blows. She had not been to blame.

Not only that, but the Grundeys' complaint about her had been dismissed as soon as SunSea head office had read Donna's report. There had been other difficult holidaymakers, but they were few and far between and Sally managed to avoid any antagonism from them. She was good at the job now.

But even if none of these things had happened, she had met Dean. Everything she did somehow revolved around him. She would never again be able to think about Greece without thinking of him.

'What are you going to do when the summer is over, Sally? Will you stay on at SunSea?'

Dean's voice made her jump, so rapt in thought had she been. Uncannily, he was echoing her own chain of thoughts.

'I don't know. I haven't decided yet. As you

know, my job with SunSea is assured, but I don't think I want to be a travel rep forever. I might design some clothes again. I've had quite a few good ideas this summer. I'll show you the sketches some time.'

Sally knew she was talking so that she did not have to contemplate that barrier, the end of the season, only a matter of weeks away. It was very sad to think of saying goodbye to Donna and Fiona, and all the other good friends she had made on Kouros. She would probably be able to see Donna back in England during the winter. But as for Dean . . .

'Hmm,' was all he said, and Sally, keeping her eyes closed, asked, 'How long will you be excavating the site here on Kouros?'

'I expect I'll stay for another year. Then it's up to me. I can move on—or keep going. Depends on whether I'm still interested.'

Sally's heart beat a little faster. If he was still here next year, and she stayed with SunSea —

'Sally, I've a suggestion to make, but I don't know if you'll like the sound of it.'

She opened her eyes as she felt him move and saw him looking down at her, raised on one elbow.

'Try me,' she suggested. 'You never know.'

'How would you feel about staying on here, with me? The reason I think you may not want to is that I know how you hate antiquities.'

'Oh, but I don't! Not any longer. I know you thought I was trying to put you off the scent at first by pretending indifference, and then you thought I was just a philistine. But I don't find them boring in the least any more. You've converted me.'

Dean smiled. 'I'm glad. Then you don't find the idea off-putting?'

'No! At least, I'm not sure . . .' Sally thought over what he was offering her. It wasn't much. He would have his work, and she would have nothing to do once the last charter flight had gone home. It would be too cold to sunbathe, and the only highlight of her day would be seeing Dean. And what would happen if he got tired of her? He wasn't offering any kind of commitment.

'You see,' she said, struggling to put it into words, 'I wouldn't have anything to do, whereas you would be busy.'

'I could think of some things for you to do,' he said, leaning down and feathering tiny kisses across her face and neck. She shivered with delight.

'I don't know,' she said, arching her neck so that he could reach the hollow of her neck. 'You're very persuasive.'

'You see,' he went on, 'I can't bear the thought of the long winter months without you, even if I knew you were coming back next summer. In fact, I can't imagine any part of my life without you now, full stop.'

'But what about your freedom,' Sally protested weakly, pushing his head away and looking into his eyes. 'You told me how important it was to you, told me not to pry, and that you didn't need anybody's help.'

'You could say that you've converted me!' Dean said. 'Besides, I was deliberately trying to keep you at arm's length because I didn't want you to get hurt. I never have met anyone who was worth giving up my freedom for— before you, that is.'

'Oh, Dean.' Sally flung her arms around his neck, her scruples melting away. 'Did I tell you I think you're wonderful? The most handsome, sexy, gorgeous—in fact, I love you.'

Dean slipped his arms underneath her and half-leaned his weight on her. 'Not yet, but you can keep telling me—I might get to believe you. But wait a minute.' He resisted the pull of her arms. 'You didn't think you were going to have a kept man, did you? You'll have to make an honest man of me. That's part of the bargain—I'm one of the ancient relics you'll be taking on. And talking of relics, I'll be expecting to get some help from you on the site.'

Sally laughed for joy. 'You mean I'll have to work to earn my keep? I'm so glad. As for being a kept man—I was thinking of working on that.'

'Well, you'll have to start practising to obey me from now on, ready for when we take our vows, OK?'

'OK,' Sally said, eyes sparkling.

'And by the way, I love you, too, my future Mrs Samuelson,' he said before he began to kiss her in earnest.